Running up the stairs, she raced to Kim's room, sickened as she saw it just as it had been.

"Kim!" she called softly . . .

Next she went along to her own room. It was empty too. Suddenly, Erica could stand it no longer. "Kim!" she cried. Her voice flared, broke, rose out of control, and she found herself gripping the gallery rail, shouting through the silent, echoing house.

"Kim! Kim! Kim!"

Hands of Terror
Jeanne Crecy

A BERKLEY MEDALLION BOOK
PUBLISHED BY
BERKLEY PUBLISHING CORPORATION

For Kristin

Published by arrangement with the author's agent

SBN 425-02174-2

BERKLEY MEDALLION BOOKS are published by
Berkley Publishing Corporation
200 Madison Avenue
New York, N.Y. 10016

BERKLEY MEDALLION BOOKS ® TM 757,375

Printed in Canada

BERKLEY MEDALLION EDITION, JUNE, 1972

I

Erica caught her first glimpse of the great house in the arcing light of the taxi as it swung round at the gate. Not a light showed in any of the dozens of windows along the front. In sudden misgiving, she called to the driver to wait, but he was too far down the drive to hear.

At least the gate was open. In the late English summer twilight, Erica peered at the intricate work on the iron grille. Hands? Yes, many of them; single and clasped, languishing, spread as if in negation, stretched in welcome, or as if in blessing. At the top of each gate column was sculpted a pair of outspread stone hands. Erica could not guess whether they offered or implored, but the silent hands communicated sadness to her.

Chilled, though the warmth of the day had lingered into night, she studied the house, unable to see more than its huge squarish shape, turreted along the roof, trailing on one side into a lower wing that lost itself among small trees, shrubs and walls. Unicorns guarded the door. On the other side of the house spread a vast open lawn with giant trees rising against the sky.

Lady Gift. The name had made her picture a smallish, graceful place, perhaps a thatched cottage set among roses and wisteria. Anyway, what she hoped would be a good job that would let her stay in England awhile, stay till she could decide what to do about Martin, waited in the dark house.

She picked up her suitcases, heavier with books than anything else, and made her overburdened way across flagstones that echoed in the stillness. Dropping the cases, she found a buzzer and rang.

No one answered. No lights came on. She pressed hard and long on the buzzer. Again there was no response.

What could be wrong? The cable from Angier Matthews had confirmed her expected train arrival time and told her to take a taxi to Lady Gift. What if she were miles from town, locked out of this house? In growing uneasiness and irritation, she leaned on the bell.

"You might as well not ring," said a clear, sweetly piercing voice.

Erica looked around but saw no one. "Do you live here?" she demanded of the unseen.

"I *stay* here." The voice came from a tree. And had to be that of a human child, playing tricks. Erica got a grip on her patience.

"Well, can you let me in?"

"The door's locked and I don't have a key."

"How will you get back inside?"

"I'll climb in through my window. But the limb would break with you, and anyway you'd be a burglar if you came that way, wouldn't you?"

Erica at that moment didn't much care what she'd be. She only wanted to be inside or on her way out of this peculiar situation.

"Are you the little girl I'm supposed to look after?" she asked.

6

"I'm not a little girl. I am nine years old and I weigh five stone."

"Then you're old enough to stop this! Climb inside at once and tell your parents I'm here!"

"I don't have parents, only Angier."

"Isn't he your father?"

"I suppose so. But he's not a proper sort of parent. And he doesn't like being disturbed after dinner."

"Disturb someone, or I shall start back to town!"

A considering silence. "That really might be best. Unless you're very nice. The last three were awful. You sound young. Are you?"

"I'm twenty-five."

"Are you pretty?"

Exasperated as Erica was, she felt a kind of admiration for the child in the tree. "Let me in and see for yourself," she challenged.

Again that contemplative stillness. Then came a slithering, scraping sound. Above Erica's head a small shadow appeared on an upper window ledge.

"Wait a few minutes and ring again," hissed the voice. "I've got to reconnect the doorbell. You won't tell on me?"

"Not if I get in right away."

Waiting, Erica reflected that at least her job wouldn't be dull. She heard a scuffling about the door, and a hoarse whisper said, "Count a hundred and ring!"

There was a running pad of feet. After a minute, Erica rang. This time the bell sounded clearly.

Within seconds a light went on. She could see through to a gallery along which a white-haired woman was hurrying to descend a heavily carved wooden staircase into the big hall. Soon she was peering through the small door window at Erica.

"Come in, dear, do!" she cried, opening the door. "You must be the American lady for Miss Kimberley. I'm Mary Shell, the housekeeper."

She took one of the suitcases and dragged it along over Erica's protest, much like a wren tugging at a giant worm, through the hall papered in gold and scarlet embossed vellum. Electric sconces lit the heavy dark furniture carved with woman-breasted beasts, strange birds and reptiles.

The main hall, past the entrance passage, vaulted upwards toward a great skylight, and a gallery ran all around the upper floor. Someone was fond of lions, for they crouched or challenged everywhere—funny Rockingham glazes, porcelain blue and white ivory, bronzes, and by the stairs, in beautifully articulated bronze, an Amazon astride a horse, spearing a lion who gripped the horse with his claws and bit on its jugular with his last savage strength.

But what struck Erica most were the hands. Carved into the polished walnut banister of the staircase, they reached out separately or intertwined, unmistakably women's hands, posed in every imaginable way, mutely saying all things.

Suddenly Erica remembered what upset her so deeply about the hands. One of those horrid stories, read as a child, that lodge deep in the mind after childish nightmares cease.

A man had carried off beautiful ladies as his brides, but once they entered his hall, he stripped them of their jewelry, and if the betrothal ring and bracelet he had given them were too tight to come off, he cut off their hands and fingers to reclaim the deadly gifts.

Mrs. Shell rested the suitcase on a stair, pushed back

her hair, and said in her distracted way, "I'll just bring your tea and biscuits to your room, shall I, or perhaps you'd enjoy soup and melon, love. What do Americans eat?"

"This American eats what she can get," laughed Erica. "But I'd rather have coffee than tea. And would you please tell Mr. Angier I'm here?"

"I'm sorry, Miss Hastings, he's not to be disturbed *ever* once he's retired to his rooms. There'll be time for you to see him in the morning."

"There must be time tonight." Erica halted on the middle landing and put down her other suitcase. "There are lots of details to be worked out, and if I don't take the job, I need to get back to the States before all the teaching jobs are filled."

"Gracious me! A night can't make all that difference, my dear. Anyway, you may rest quite easy that Mr. Angier intends to engage you. He's desperate about Miss Kim."

"But perhaps I won't care to be engaged," Erica pointed out, more calmly than she felt. "Really, if he won't see me now, I shall phone for a taxi and go back to town."

"Oh, dear, he'll be so upset!" The pink-cheeked older woman fluttered her hands and fairly wailed. "Either way, he'll be angry! Please, Miss—"

"What's the row?" came a deep voice from above.

Erica looked past the carved hands to a massive-shouldered big man with tousled black hair showing streaks of white. A pipe stuck out of the breast pocket of a tweed jacket with leather elbow patches.

Imposing as the house was, he seemed, in a rough, careless way, to dominate it. Erica could sympathize with Mary Shell's timidity at rousing him, but she returned his gaze and spoke more loudly than usual.

"I'm Erica Hastings, Mr. Matthews. I must talk with you about—"

"Must?" Heavy dark brows rose above grey eyes.

"Yes!" declared Erica.

He lounged forward, peering up. "Isn't that a bit positive before you even get to the top of the stairs?"

"Certain things must be settled, and tonight, or I'll only need the stairs for going down." Erica was more emphatic than she would have been had his presence not been so intimidating. She was sure that if he routed her now, she would have an impossible time standing up to him later. Taking a deep breath, she looked straight into his eyes. "I—I'd rather be positive at the start, Mr. Matthews, than negative at the end!"

Their gazes locked while Mary Shell made small despairing noises. Erica was sure that her hair had gone to tangles from the damp and her lipstick must have vanished long ago. She was further certain that this man had noted all that; she felt, in fact, as if she were being examined through a microscope, and stared back defiantly.

He was used to having his own way. If she let him bully her now, he always would. Better lose the job before it began! He seemed to relax all at once, actually smiling. Mary Shell drew an audible breath of relief.

"Well, Miss American Erica, come into my study and let's make our arrangements, so I can get back to work. I hope you do realize that I work at night." He looked at the two suitcases as if he wished he hadn't seen them, but gathered them up and went along the hall to an open door through which he thrust the luggage.

"Mrs. Shell," he ordered, "make dinner for Miss

Hastings to be eaten in half an hour." Scowling suddenly, he turned to the nervous little housekeeper.

"Where was Peggie tonight? I told her we were expecting Miss Hastings and to be on the watch for her."

Mrs. Shell twisted her hands. "I—I think Peggie's not well, sir. I'm sure she's not!"

"You mean she decided to go strolling with a boyfriend," Angier Matthews said. "If you want to keep the girl, Mrs. Shell, she must do her duty before she has her fun!"

"Yes, sir, I'll tell her, sir!" Mary Shell bobbed her head and trotted down the gallery.

He held a door for Erica. She almost felt him rushing her through it, and moved with deliberation, looking around the long, high-ceilinged room. Three walls were bookshelves from top to bottom. A draperied window was in the middle of the fourth wall, and on either side were velvet-covered panels covered with playbills, pictures of play scenes, characters, photos of Angier on opening nights. In most he was alone, but in a few earlier ones, he smiled into the upturned face of a beautiful woman.

Displayed around the walls and inset in the bookshelves were masks, some very old, fixed in the comedy smile or tragic frown of Greek drama; others shamanistic, primitive things trimmed with feathers, fur, teeth and claws. And there were fantastic modern masks, wistful unicorns, Mephistos, Undines; and death masks.

"They aren't the originals," he said, touching one of Balzac and slightly rearranging one of Trotsky next to Dante's hard jaw and humped nose. "But I've had casts made when possible and got the others from an artist who specializes in such creations. I find masks wonderful things, Miss Hastings."

He picked up a woman's mask of silver and held it to her face so that she felt the cold metal. "If you were to wear that till it seemed your own face, would it change you to Medea? Or this Gorgon's face, would it make you deadly?"

Was he a little mad?

Erica spoke through the pressure of the metal. "I think it more likely that I would change the mask!"

He laughed and there was an easing in his manner as he took the mask away. "Well done, Miss America!" He pronounced it so that it sounded like Am-Erica. "I suppose you'd agree to having your face done? See, even Mary Shell is here."

The housekeeper's face smiled in gentle bewilderment, and there were other masks that looked more like real people than deified celebrities or characters.

"I *shall* want your mask," he decided, turning Erica's head and gazing at her profile. His hand was strong but the touch was impersonal. "Those cheekbones—the proud chin—have you any Indian blood?"

"I'm Heinz 57 varieties, American mix," she said, though she was mostly Welsh, Scotch and Irish, the rebel Gaelic bloods, with tinges of French and Dutch. Somehow the result in her of these solid strains had been a faintly exotic look, strongly marked eyebrows, almost Mongolian cheekbones, and a full mouth which she often wished smaller.

Egyptian, Martin had called her, softening it usually to 'Gyptian. . . . Well, that and Martin were far away.

"I don't want my mask made, Mr. Matthews."

"Why not?"

She gazed around at the expressions that watched her from ivory, plaster, silver, bronze, wood, copper. "I don't know. It just makes me uneasy."

"I wouldn't make it a condition of employment," he said, with his first real smile. "But I hope you'll come round to it."

He sank down in a crimson leather monk's chair at a battered, much polished trestle table spread with manuscripts, pencils, pens, books. One mask faced him—the beautiful face of the woman in the pictures. The ceramic was as warmly tinted as the famous Nefertiti Erica had once seen on holiday in Berlin's Dahlem Museum.

Every time Angier set to work, he looked into those smiling eyes, faced the calm beauty. Who was she? Someone surely greatly loved. A question struck Erica like a pang.

Had the mask been made from a dead or living face?

The master of this room motioned Erica to sit. "Now then," he said briskly, "what are these urgent matters that won't wait till morning?"

"I'm confused about exactly what I'm to do."

"Tutor-companion? That seems plain enough." He spoke in an arbitrary tone that suggested he was far from clear himself, and made an almost shooing motion with his hand. "Just do what you'd do if you were Kimberley's mother. Always assuming, of course, that you aren't a child-batterer. See she does her studies, has little parties, her buttons are on and her hair clean—that she brushes her teeth and has clean fingernails. That kind of thing."

And that she doesn't climb out of her room nights to greet strangers or disconnect doorbells, Erica thought.

"I'd do my best. Now about vacations—"

He raised his brows. "Do mothers take vacations?"

"If they don't, they should," Erica said firmly. "And I must go to the States now and then to see my mother. She is in a nursing home and her health is poor." It was none of his business that the home was a private hospital for mental patients.

"So? I advertised for an unencumbered person on purpose to avoid any conflict of loyalties."

He leaned back and considered her a moment. She looked back steadily though her palms were wet. He offered a good salary, which was needed for her mother's care, but she could not let him steamroller over her.

"So you won't have a mask made and you insist on vacations to visit your sick mother," he said in a reflective way with just a hint of sarcasm. "What other awkwardness am I to expect?"

"I shall need time off—"

"You can arrange afternoons with Peggie or Mrs. Shell. When Kim is in school, from the time she is left till the time she's collected, you may do what you please, but you will be on duty from her waking to her going to bed, and her summer holidays have just started so you'll have almost two months of concentrated time with her. Your room will adjoin hers in case she needs you. Of course you must get a British driving license as soon as possible so you can take her about. It would be best to have a half-hour lesson daily. My secretary will arrange it. When you feel competent, you'll chauffeur Kim."

"Mr. Matthews," persisted Erica, more from principle than desire, "I really should have a regular night out."

14

"Boyfriend?"

"No, but there might be. And plays, concerts and so on are not on in the day."

"Work it out with Mrs. Shell. It will be your responsibility to see that Kim is never on her own evenings. I work then and can't be interrupted." He gave a disgruntled laugh. "Tonight's exception must not become a rule! Ordinarily when I close that door, consider me dead! And don't dream of calling me unless it demands resurrection!"

"I don't see why I should need to trouble you if I have reasonable freedom to make decisions."

"You do. As long as the decisions *are* reasonable. Then you'll take the position?"

His face, in that moment, seemed a mask, too, and for some reason Erica had a flash vision of those hands along the banister, a thrill of warning. But he had agreed to her terms. She should at least make a trial.

"Yes," Erica said. "I'll do my best."

"Good." He glanced at his watch. "Your food should be ready. If you have other questions, Miss Hastings, settle them with my secretary and accountant; they'll both be in early in the morning." He swiveled his chair and spoke with slow emphasis which she found infuriating. "Remember that my accountant, secretary and staff are here to save me worry and time. So are you. Do your duties with that always in mind." He rose as if resenting a courtesy he felt constrained to offer, and opened the door. "Good night, Miss Hastings."

She could almost feel his hand in the middle of her back, shoving her into the hall. His sacrosanct time! He needn't worry, she wouldn't bother him again! Let him stay shut up with those masks for company!

15

Erica saw Mrs. Shell beckoning from the gallery and followed her to the kitchen.

"Here, love, nice Lancashire hot pot, a bit of trifle with cream, and coffee. Will you have it in your room?"

"I'll eat in the kitchen and save fuss," said Erica. Mrs. Shell set her lips in disapproval at this lack of decorum and began washing a basin of cauliflower with great energy.

"Is the little girl in bed?" Erica asked, finishing off the stinging-hot meat and potato casserole. She soothed her mouth with coffee and the trifle which could have been all desserts to all men—cake in the bottom, custard next, then raspberry jello topped with whipped cream, nuts and glacé cherries.

"Miss Kim goes to bed at nine sharp, Miss Erica, and I pray that you'll continue the rule. Are you used to children?"

"I've taught in high school for three years."

"You'll find that quite different from teaching Miss Kim manners," predicted Mrs. Shell, with satisfied gloom. "If you've finished, let me show you to your room."

II

In a bay between two large bow windows stood a huge bed canopied in old rose satin stitched with silver. The walls were creamy ivory with gilt leaves and roses bordering the ceiling. A graceful chaise longue with a silver swan worked into the frame was upholstered in brilliant turquoise, but otherwise it was a room of silver, ivory and rose.

A chandelier of enameled roses from buds to full-grown flowers, interwoven with silver stems and crystal leaves, hung in the center of the slightly domed ceiling. The three-sided bay opposite the bed was mirrored from floor to wall with built-in ivory wardrobes and chests spread from either side. On the left, a door opened to a bath done in silver and turquoise.

"This can't be my room!" Erica protested.

"It adjoins Miss Kimberley's," said Mrs. Shell, with a primming of her lips. "The other bedrooms are on the other side of the gallery."

Erica looked about her, troubled and almost oppressed by the luxurious femininity. It was a room for costly mistresses or adored, pampered wives; not a place for a teacher who had taught by choice in a Houston, Texas, slum school; not a place for the hired help.

"Was—was this Miss Kim's mother's room?" The question forced itself out of Erica's uneasiness, her sense of being an interloper, a trespasser.

"Yes, it was." Mrs. Shell folded up the quilted satin coverlet, turned back the bed. "Good night, Miss Erica."

"Where is Mrs. Matthews?"

"She's dead."

"Oh! How—how long has it been?"

Mrs. Shell plumped the ruffled pillows and turned with finality. "It happened when Kim was a baby. Please don't ask about it, Miss Hastings. It makes Mr. Matthews terribly upset."

"But this room—Isn't there another I could use?"

"Not near Miss Kimberley," said the housekeeper. "Never mind, you'll get used to it. Mr. Matthews had it all done as a wedding surprise for Mrs. Matthews, some famous decorator stayed here six months fussing and complaining the whole time. But it *is* beautiful. I should think you'd be pleased!" Before Erica could object or raise more questions, Mrs. Shell gave her a pat on the shoulder and vanished.

Erica got out her night things. She opened the closets, hesitated at the empty rose-satin quilted hangers. She caught a glimpse of a face in the mirror and scarcely recognized her own pale reflection for one frightened moment.

Had she looked like that with Angier, hair all blown and tangled, lipstick gone? She laughed, forcing herself to relax. At least he couldn't think she had tried to blandish him! She undressed quickly, put on pajamas, brushed her hair, and carried her toiletries into the bathroom.

The shell-shaped ivory tub had fittings of silver

swans while the soap dishes were silver shells. The walls were tiled translucent turquoise and the thick, soft towels and rug were rose.

In spite of a scolding Puritan conscience, Erica would not have resisted a sensuous reveling delight in the luxurious beauty if the room had simply been for guests; but she could not banish a constant awareness of the other woman who had moved about this room, watched her face and body in the triple mirror, bathed in the shell, crossed to the high bed and settled into lavender-scented sheets and pillows.

Was Angier's wife the woman of the lovely mask?

Erica got up, feet sinking into the fleecy rug, and slipped behind the draperies to peer out the window. Mist had rolled up till only the closer trees stood dark against it. One patch of light showed on the lawn and she thought it must be from Angier's study. A shadow moved across the light, a distorting mass on the square below. Erica shivered and got back in the high bed.

A strange man, locking himself apart even in this richly sumptuous home. He was used to ruling absolutely, but it didn't seem to have made him happy. Erica remembered the voice from the tree and smiled with a sudden lift of heart.

The little girl was lively; her father hadn't quelled her! And there wouldn't be much need to see Angier or be affected by him. It was a good job, paying enough to give her mother the best care. And as for not liking this room—well, how silly could she get? The room was there, not being used, and it plainly made sense for her to be near Kim. The sense of being an intruder would surely fade as she got used to the room and had her own things about.

But it was so dark!

She sprang out of bed again, yanked the drapery pulls. The mist was close to the windows now, but still the room lightened a bit. It was not the close constricting black that it had been with the draperies pulled.

That's enough foolishness, she told herself, and for the third time, got back under the canopy.

She was floating into sleep when a clock somewhere struck one. She roused long enough to wonder if they were near a church, then sank into heavy slumber.

She woke with instant warning which made her lie still, open her eyes cautiously, just enough to see. A figure was by her, leaning close.

Fear choked Erica. Should she scream? *Could* she? Her throat had that sick weak feeling it got in nightmares when she tried to cry out and couldn't.

This was no nightmare. Someone—something was there.

A detached part of Erica's mind worked on in spite of her terror. A scream might not bring speedy help—and she was far from sure she could scream loud enough to be heard. She had no idea of what the figure intended; it might go away, but not knowing what it was was unthinkable, unbearable.

So she did the only thing that seemed possible—gathered herself and lunged at the presence. She heard a gasp, caught a wrist, knew she was dealing with a woman or a very small man, certainly with flesh and blood, as they fell to the floor.

"Stop!" Hands were planted in Erica's chest, pushing at her. "Let go! I wasn't going to hurt you!"

Erica switched on the bedside lamp. A brilliantly handsome woman scrambled up from the floor clutching an emerald robe about her, eyes bright with anger and fright. She looked at her wrists which were scratched and welted, narrowed her gaze.

"You act a wild beast! But then you are American!"

Shocked into laughter, Erica retorted, "I suppose invading a stranger's bedroom is proper English behavior?"

"I only wanted to see what you looked like!"

That brought the exchange back to facts.

"Who are you?" Erica demanded.

A cold sensation ran down her spine but she instantly rejected it. This full-breasted woman whose slanting eyes blazed out of a triangular witch-beautiful face was no dainty ghost; she was, in her way, as out of key with this room as was Erica. And she was hotly, richly, proudly flesh and blood.

"Do you live here?" Erica persisted. "Are you the secretary?"

"That cow?" The wide mouth drew into a circle of disdain. "Certainly not! Her room is in the servants' quarters! I live in the main house!"

She stared at Erica in direct challenge, but there was something so childlike in her willful capriciousness that Erica could not take her too seriously, smiled and shrugged.

"If you live here, I'll eventually learn who you are and what you do—so please go along now and let me sleep."

The woman drew herself up with an affronted hiss, her long neck arched like an aggressive swan's. "I am Caitlyn St. Clair!"

"I'm sure I've seen the name, but—"

"Barbarian! I have played leading lady in all Angier's good plays!"

21

"The others were bad because you weren't in them?"

"I wasn't in them because they were bad! Angier is such a fool! Writing these dull tedious things people don't want to see! He has to do a play for me—a role I can interpret as I did his first play, the one that made us both!"

"I thought all Angier Matthews' plays did pretty well," said Erica.

"A holdover from the brilliance of the first ones—the ones he wrote for me!" Caitlyn St. Clair came closer, green eyes blazing, and Erica almost envied her the ability to get so worked up over anything. "I have come down here to show him that he must abandon this ridiculous trend of hashed-over Ibsen and produce another great play that I can burn into the souls of people—something to stab their vitals. But that secretary—she thinks he should write about wildcat strikes and overcrowded colored emigrants and a floating pound! Angier's gift is pure creation, not social messages! And the stars tie our careers together! Neither can thrive alone!" She squinted suspiciously at Erica. "You don't have any political ideas, I hope? You won't put more crazy slogans into Angier's mind?"

"I have only seen him once, Miss St. Clair, but I don't think anyone can put much in his mind that isn't already there!"

The actress gnawed her lower lip, cast Erica a smoldering glance, then caught her hands with placating zeal.

"Oh, I have been naughty! Do forgive me!" She laughed, and the sudden lilting supplication was impossible for Erica to repulse though she remained puzzled and on guard. "We must be friends—you'll see what I mean! That secretary! And Angier! So when we meet tomorrow, it will be new, for the first occasion!" She squeezed Erica's hands again and ran lightly out.

Dazed, Erica locked the door, left on a small night light, and went to bed for what seemed the hundredth time.

Only as she nestled gratefully into the pillows did she remember that Caitlyn had never said *why* she had crept in; in spite of the actress's childish spontaneity, there could be a deranged or malevolent mind at work behind those brilliant eyes. And the secretary who was to give Erica her instructions in the morning—would she be as peculiar?

Sufficient to the night is the evil thereof—Erica thought sleepily. Of course if it proved to be an utter madhouse, she could leave. Tomorrow should tell. . . .

She woke at the sound of a tap on the door, followed by a louder one. Unlocking, she saw Mrs. Shell bearing a tray. "Here's your tea, Miss Hastings. Breakfast is at nine. You'll meet Miss Kim then."

"Thank you," said Erica.

To tea or not to tea? She hated to do anything to put Mrs. Shell off but it seemed foolish to begin something she would need to halt. With her best smile, Erica said, "You needn't bring tea in the mornings, Mrs. Shell. Coffee at breakfast is all I need."

"Perhaps a Horlick's?" hazarded Mrs. Shell, obviously thrown off balance by anyone's not wanting morning tea. "Ovaltine? Bovril?"

Erica shook her head each time, and each time Mrs. Shell looked more disappointed, till at last Erica succumbed. "Orange juice would be lovely, if it's not too much trouble."

"I'll bring it," Mrs. Shell said, with an air that implied it was great trouble, but still her duty.

Erica dressed quickly, downed the orange juice that had appeared while she was in the bath, made her bed and went out to face the household.

A woman whose face looked older than a figure showed to oversmug advantage by cable-patterned tights and a plaid mini, rose from her place at the round table to offer her hand and say, as she studied Erica, "I'm Sybil Johnson, Mr. Matthews' secretary." She had ash blonde hair pulled up in a chignon. "Did you rest well your first night at Lady Gift?"

Glancing along the table to Caitlyn and a tall bronzed man who stood and introduced himself as Malcolm Harrow, the business secretary and accountant, Erica said, "I was too excited to rest well, but I suppose it takes a while to get used to new places."

Caitlyn scowled. Sybil looked pleasantly interested, and Malcolm Harrow choked on toast and laughter.

"Some places you never get used to, Miss Hastings! For instance, this is the first morning in six months that Caitlyn has joined us for breakfast!"

"Yes, you are up early, aren't you, dear," murmured Sybil. "I do hope you're feeling well!"

"I'm studying a role," muttered Caitlyn, taking more marmalade.

"Oh, a new one?" Sybil raised slim patrician eyebrows even higher than her horn rims. "How marvelous! Will you be going back to London?"

"Not until Angier does!"

Malcolm Harrow smiled cozily at both women. As Erica sat down, there was a swift pelt of running steps. Sybil Johnson smiled at the runner and said, "Miss Hastings, this is Kimberley. Kim, leave Miss Hastings room to breathe!"

For Kimberley, after shaking Erica's hand and bending one knee, had pushed her chair up close, as if staking a claim on her person, and reached for a box of one of the sugared, puffed cereals that Erica had fervently hoped would never leave the United States.

Long straight hair of glossy chestnut had Kimberley, and clear grey eyes that stared meditatively into space except when they riveted on someone with an intentness that produced almost physical shock. Flawless elf-child skin and a quick, delighted smile that turned her long, narrow face bewitching made her the most attractive child Erica had ever seen.

"Mr. Matthews often breakfasts in his room," Sybil explained. "I have notes on different things you'll need to know about Kimberley. Right now she's on summer holiday till the seventeenth of September. She needs some coaching in her tables and fractions—a good chance for you to learn the English weights and measures if you don't know them. Mr. Matthews also wants her to read aloud a half hour daily, and she should have a swim and either a brisk walk or cycling—exercise, you know. Once a week he expects a three- or four-page essay on a subject of your choosing, and it will be up to you to see she has plenty of informational reading as well as books for pleasure.

"Of course you will be responsible for her appearance, clothing, and general grooming, too."

"That makes me sound like a horse," grumbled

Kimberley. She had been taking in all of Sybil Johnson's outline with deep attention and now screwed up her face, regarding Erica as if strongly considering freeing herself from this bond servant with tutelary powers.

"Angier said you would be company!" she complained. "It sounds more like you'll be a teacher. Ugh!"

"Your papa should send you off to boarding school," said Caitlyn. "Then you could stay with the mistresses in summer instead of needing all kinds of arrangements at Lady Gift! I'm always telling Angier it's no place for a child! Especially an Aries!"

Behind her hand, Kimberley stuck out her tongue at the actress. Erica decided not to assume responsibility at that moment.

"I don't want to be a boarder," Kimberley said. "They get only three shillings and sixpence a week pocket money, they have to go to bed early and have prayers every night, and only get high tea for dinner! Fourth formers get studies of their own and then it might be all right, but I shan't board till I can have a study."

"Children," said Caitlyn, "belong at school."

"Actresses," retorted Kimberley, "belong on the stage. You can't act down here at Lady Gift. When are you going back to London?"

Caitlyn gasped, Malcolm chuckled, and Sybil put in quickly, "That's naughty of you, Kimberley! Never ask questions people may find it awkward to answer." She beamed at the actress who clattered a buttery knife and got to her feet.

"There you go poisoning everybody's mind!" she flamed at Sybil. "If you'd leave Angier alone, he'd

26

write my play and I could get back to London! Sow! Bitch! Secretary!"

Sybil cocked her head. "There's something wrong with your cadence," she declared. "And your logic's worse. Caitlyn, love, disabuse yourself of the notion that I'm sabotaging you with Angier! Far from it. But really, you should realize that he could do the play far better if you weren't breathing down his neck. It rankles, darling! If you keep on like this, he may never do the play at all!"

"Just because you were married to him once and still have a share in all his copyrights, you think you can control what he creates! You're a fuzzy bookkeeper of a Virgoan!"

"I'm the bookkeeper," said Malcolm, "but I'm a Leo, which should make me a leader."

"You were born on the cusp," retorted Caitlyn. "Don't try to change the subject! This Virgoan, this—this secretary—"

Sybil shook her head. "Caitlyn, Caitlyn! That was long ago, if not far away. I was Angier's secretary before our marriage and am the only person who can thoroughly understand his very complex business. If we find it possible to carry on, you should admire rather than attack the relationship." She smiled benignly. "Of course, I suppose you simply can't comprehend how two people, once intimate, can keep up a friendly, close, yet platonic association."

Caitlyn's face contorted. "Sec—secretary!" she shouted, and ran from the room.

Sybil stirred brown Demerara sugar into her coffee and shook her head. "I'm sorry, Miss Hastings. You'll think we're frightful!"

"Caitlyn is," said Kimberley. "Sybil, I didn't know

you and Angier were ever married!"

"It was a long time ago," Sybil said. She gave Kim's cheek a light touch. "We had worked together so long there seemed no reason not to marry—but when your papa met your pretty mama, there was every reason to end it. Your mama and I were the best of friends, child. It's nothing to work around in that funny fretty mind of yours!" She smiled again at Erica and rose. "Well, I've a stacked-up desk after being off yesterday. Do let me know about any problems, Erica. I'll be your liaison with Angier."

"And you had better believe that!" said Malcolm Harrow. He had a handsome carved look like a bronze falcon, his nose slightly hooked, head aristocratic and poised, with his hair trimmed in layers as precise as a bird's feathers.

"I'll arrange credit at any shops you'll use often to buy things for Kim. You can spend for the child within reason, but major purchases should first be approved by Mr. Matthews or Miss Johnson." He gave Kim a considering, mock-stern look. "Have a successful day, Kimberley. Don't spring all your tricks at once on Miss Hastings! Remember she's a fellow countrywoman!"

"Half-countrywoman," corrected Kimberley. "I'm half-English." She cast Erica a ravishingly smug smile. "But I have dual citizenship. Isn't that good?"

"Wonderful!" assured Erica. "The best of both worlds!"

But as she walked along the gallery, with the child gripping her hand much as if Erica were a jealously treasured new possession, Erica thought the world this child inhabited, watching it all with those grey direct

28

eyes, was a strange one indeed, the kingdom of Angier Matthews with his vassals jostling for advantage.

Thank goodness, her work was with Kimberley. It should be possible to keep free of the tangles and undercurrents between the others.

III

"You didn't tell on me," Kimberley exulted as they walked along the picture-hung gallery. "About my locking you out and hiding in the tree, I mean. I'm so glad you didn't!"

Erica laughed. "I doubt you would have been punished very severely."

"Oh, that's not it," said Kimberley. "I'm glad because I can trust you." She stopped at the carved rail of the gallery, cushioned her chin on her hands and stared at the floor of the lower hall thirty feet below, where rays from the skylight jeweled a Persian rug.

"You can trust most people," Erica assured her.

"No, you can't," retorted Kimberley. She continued to brood. "Caitlyn tried to throw herself over this rail once, but Angier dragged her back."

"That was lucky."

The child looked doubtful. "Sybil says Caitlyn will kill herself sooner or later unless she's locked up. She and Malcolm both think Caitlyn is in cloud-cuckoo land, except she's not happy. Do *you* think she's out of her mind?"

Erica spoke with great care. She was going to have to watch what she said in front of this child, so ready to hear and absorb.

"She seems easily upset and rather intense. But that's more normal for an actress than not, I should think."

Kimberley glanced up in that quick way she had. "Do you like Angier?"

"I haven't had time to like anyone yet," evaded Erica. "Except you!"

The child's arms shot around her in a surprisingly tight hug. "Oh, I'm glad! Because I do so like you! Must I call you Miss Hastings?"

"So long as your father doesn't mind, I'd rather you called me Erica."

"He doesn't care what I do so long as I'm nice around him, look pretty, do well at school, and especially don't make too much noise," said Kim, with devastating frankness. "Nobody here really cares about me except Peg. Can I take you about Lady Gift or—" she made a face—"do I have to study first?"

"Show me where you are in your math and what you're reading. Then I can think about it while you show me around."

"That'll be splendid!" Kim glowed. "And I really will do my lessons just as soon as we're back!"

The child's room was curiously decorated for a girl of her age—still done with fairy tale and nursery motifs. Stuffed animals almost covered the Pooh quilt; dolls filled the floor-to-ceiling shelves, stocking dolls, china-headed ones, jointed wooden ones, round Russian nesting ones. Cradles and beds were filled with baby dolls, swaddled or in nightgowns or play clothes, sitting in high chairs or in a playpen—a family of baby dolls.

Kimberley hugged one, straightened another. "I'm their mother," she told Erica. "These are my children down here where I play." She held up a beautiful but

31

bedraggled doll in a fraying satin robe. "This is Lady Margaret. She sleeps with me. The ones on the shelf are too nice to play with. Angier brings them from places he visits."

"They're quite wonderful," Erica said, but she gazed at the astonishing collection in resentment that came near to anger. It was so much easier to give dolls than an hour of reading or playing games—so much easier to give unique souvenirs than concern and love.

"I like those I can play with best," confided Kimberley. "I make up stories with them and act out tragedies and comedies."

With less enthusiasm Kimberley showed her math book and dragged from under the bed a startling array of books—a battered edition of Dracula, biographies of Beethoven, Catherine of Russia and Elizabeth I, several Peanuts paperbacks, Enid Blyton mysteries, and some dog-eared worn books about horses and tropical fish.

"You must like horses," Erica said.

"I do, but Angier says I'm allergic. He says I can ride sometimes at the stable. I don't like that! I want my own horse. He got me the fish instead."

Between pride and melancholy, Kim pulled the folding door across a windowed bay. A long tank glittered, decked with coral, plants, and fish that finned in and out.

"There's Othello and Desdemona." Kim pointed to a pair of striped, miniature-eel-like creatures. "He killed his mate when we brought them home by slicing her gill, so we bought another girl for him. Prince Charlie is the little catfish, he's my favorite. See how he goes up so cute? Those clear ones are black widows, the striped are zebras, those orange ones are tiger barbs, and thos⌐

are platies and swordtails. The black mollies are all babies of the big mama, Fatso. Look, I can hand-feed her!"

She demonstrated. The creature, a tiny whale, gulped at the surface and ate the flakes. Kim replaced the top.

"I had some most beautiful tetras!" she said mournfully. "They glowed with red in their eyes and tails—but one of the swordtails killed them all. We had to take him back to the shop. They die if the temperature drops, and they get white spots and do all kinds of things. I'm always worried about them. But if I tell Angier, he'll want to get rid of them. And I do want *something* alive!"

"But why not a cat or dog?"

"I'm allergic to them—and birds, too. And smog! That's why we don't live in London." Kim paused for tragic effect and whispered, "and I'm allergic to chocolate! I don't even like any other candy! It's *torture* to watch everyone else wolfing down those lovely mints and things when I can't have them! I hope you don't like chocolate, Erica."

"I do," Erica confessed, "but I can't have it."

"You can't?" Kim looked positively radiant. "Are you allergic?"

"In a way, perhaps." Erica pointed to her nose. "It's an awful certainty that if I have a chocolate, a great ugly spot will pop out right there! And it lasts for days. So I never have chocolate."

"I wouldn't mind the spot," said Kim, embracing Erica to celebrate this new bond. "And I'm sorry you can't have the candy—but I'm glad you won't eat it in front of me! Peg loves me but she gobbles chocolate! Now let's go down!"

Outside the house, unicorns in weathered stone guarded the main entrance, and heavy wisteria twined up to the second floor, purpling one side of the great house, in its second blooming, Kim said. Geraniums and begonias in every shade of red, pink and violet grew in grey stone troughs under the windows and were spaced along the main drive in huge bowls six feet round set on raised platforms of crazy-paving.

As they walked toward the side where giant magnolias rose to the roof, the air was heavy with the sweet odor. "That vine is outside our windows. It's beautiful when it blooms in May," Kim said. "Big pigeons nest there. Did you hear them last night?"

"No, but I'm glad to be on the alert for them," said Erica. The house had enough nerve-wracking possibilities without concocting terror from bird sounds! "How old is Lady Gift?"

"This house is only about a hundred years, Angier says. It's built to look like the first two, which burned down. See that wall, and the little buildings? They go back to Elizabethan days. See that acacia? It was planted during Cromwell's rebellion to show Royalists could have refuge here. One did stay," said Kim, matter-of-factly, "and that's when the place was first burned down."

The house sat in acres of parkland with trees Kim named as rich maroon copper beeches, limes, chestnuts and a mixture of holly, firs, cedars, oaks and maples.

One tremendous tree dominated the south lawn, a hundred feet high at least, with giant layered limbs.

"That is the cedar of Lebanon," pointed Kim. "A crusader brought it back, one of the barons who made

King John agree to Magna Carta. It's the biggest tree at Lady Gift."

She led the way around, introducing the trees as if they were people. "This monkey puzzle tree survives from the time of dinosaurs. The squills really do look like tails, don't they! And that lovely gnarly one is a deodar from the Himalayas. Now just come under here—" She led Erica beneath the low-trained limbs of a giant Douglas fir.

"It's like a vault—a house under the limbs!" Erica looked up and about, catching her breath in delighted wonder. "You must play here a lot!"

"I do, there's a good place to sit right in the crotch," said Kim. She climbed into the split of four thick trunks, all united at the base and then spreading into the vast, needle-floored tree shelter which must have arched over a diameter of fifty feet. "You can come here any time you like," she invited. "Snow never gets under here and even rain doesn't get through very much. But I still haven't shown you my favorite tree!"

Scrambling off the mossy trunk, Kim caught Erica's hand and burst from under the great fir. They came straight upon a frondy graceful small tree with weeping branches that cascaded to the ground, making an oval umbrella.

Eyes sparkling, Kimberley pulled Erica inside. Soft green light filtered through to unmown grass beneath the protecting skirts of the dainty, elegant little tree. It was cool and very still.

"This is the wych elm," Kim said. "Isn't she a darling? It's always ten degrees cooler here, and the men don't mow under the boughs so wild flowers love it. You're too late for the primroses and buttercups, but next year you can see them."

Next they came to a wide strip of assorted flowers, ranging in height from tall white lilies in the back to zinnias and sweet william in front, running the length of a mellow brick-walled garden. Kim called it a herbaceous border.

Beyond was a soft fruit frame for raspberries and gooseberries. The wall curved around an open summer pavilion, stacked now with faggots of wood. The wall led into an orchard.

Small apples burdened some trees but others were grown over with twisting ivy, which forced the trunks into goitered knots; limbs like mutilated arms were broken off where vines had finally choked them to death. It was a strange contrast to the perfectly kept grounds.

"What a shame!" cried Erica, pulling at one tightly gripping growth of ivy. "Why don't they prune these?"

"Angier says the trees are too old. He's going to have them taken out," mourned Kimberley. "Mind those nettles! They'll sting!"

But Erica was already drawing back from a smarting along one arm and hand.

"Let me put dock leaf on it," said Kim, and rubbed the red marks. "The orchard is full of nettles so it's not nice to walk through. That's too bad because I love it here. In the spring the trees get thick with white blossoms and the bees are so happy!"

"What happens to the fruit?" Erica asked, for even in their neglected state the trees were covered with apples.

"Most just fall and rot."

Erica bit back a shocked exclamation. After all, it was none of her business. But she felt sad about the neglected trees as they passed through another gate into a walled garden which covered several acres.

"This is the new orchard." Kim pointed to young, carefully tended trees. "Those vines are black currants, and pears and plums are espaliered along that wall to get all the sun. We still have lots of peas and broad beans, and runner beans will be ready soon. Pigeons ate the cabbage, that's why the scarecrows are up." Words tumbled out in her haste to share her knowledge with an interested listener. "Those are greenhouses for cucumbers and tomatoes, and strawberries were in that lot of frames."

She led Erica through a gate in the other end of the garden that opened into a patio surrounding a free-form swimming pool. Beyond the pool was a tennis court next to a rose garden where two men were at work. Another was astride a mower like a small tractor, looping in careful swirls over the vast lawns. Erica wondered again at the difference between the beautifully kept main grounds and the dying orchard—shut away almost as if in disgrace, perishing in the slow grip of the ivy, overgrown with nettles—yet lovely, somehow.

"How did Lady Gift come by its name?" Erica asked.

"Oh, it was called that from the start, even before Cromwell's men burned it down the first time," explained Kim, at once carried away. "It was built as a dower house when an Earl's daughter, who was known for her beautiful hands, married a dark handsome gentleman from Cornwall, and it was called Lady Gift because it was what she brought to her marriage. The couple seemed happy, especially when they had a baby boy. But a time came when the Earl heard nothing from his daughter, Lady Margaret, for quite a while. He got worried and came to see her."

Kim paused, eyes round with the suspense of her own story. "Everyone was gone but the baby and its old nurse. She had to tell the Earl a terrible thing. The Cornish gentleman thought his wife had a lover and tried to make her confess. He had that jealous Spanish blood, you see, of men shipwrecked in the defeat of the Armada. She held out her lovely hands, begging him to be kind, and he struck them off with his sword. She bled to death, protesting her innocence, and he rode off like a madman. No one ever knew what happened to him, though the Earl sent trusted men to bring him back to vengeance if he could be found. The Earl raised the baby, who later was master of Lady Gift, and in memory of the wronged lady, her father had her hands carved on the banisters and gates, and they're around the base of her effigy in the cathedral in town."

Erica shivered. "That's quite a history!"

"It's more than history," said Kim, quite swept up in the tale, lowering her voice for an eerie effect that was funny in its exaggeration. "Each time the house has been burned, that banister has been saved even when nothing else can be got out. And Peg says—" Kim broke off, frowning at Erica. "Do you think Peg ought to tell me ghost stories?"

"She plainly has," said Erica, with resignation.

"Yes. Well, Peg says she's seen the Lady walking along the gallery, looking for her hands. And she says—everybody says—they can hear a horseman thunder down the drive some nights, and though they don't see anyone, they hear the hooves and a voice cursing in Spanish."

"Mmm," teased Erica. "Strange they hear one ghost and see the other, isn't it?"

"You don't believe it?"

"I'll believe it when I see—or hear it."

Kim gave her another of those wild, impetuous hugs. "I'm glad of that! You see, when Peg tells the stories I just *have* to listen, but then I can't get to sleep, and I think I hear someone walking but I'm afraid to look. Peg sleeps outside my door but she'd make fun or scare me worse, and I don't dare bother Angier at night."

"You can come in to me if you get jumpy," Erica said. "But you mustn't use it as an excuse for staying up!"

Another of those breathless hugs. "Oh, you're nice, Erica! I promise! I won't come unless I'm just petrified!"

They walked on, hands joined. *A strange life for a child*, Erica thought, and inevitably, *poor little rich girl!*

A long brick building was topped by a bell which struck eleven. "That's the Clock House," said Kim. "The staff lives there, the three gardeners and their families, Mrs. Shell and Peg."

"When do you usually have your swim?" asked Erica.

"Angier swims at four and I go with him if I haven't already been, with Caitlyn or Sybil or Malcolm. Would you like to go in now while it's warm? It could cloud over and be nasty out in an hour." She nodded toward a narrow white building at the side of the patio. "My suit's in the dressing room."

"A swim would be nice," said Erica. "I'll have to unpack my suit, so don't get in till I'm back."

"Oh, I won't!" promised Kimberley and danced toward the dressing stalls.

In minutes, Erica was back with her perennial moss-green jersey maillot that simply would not wear out. She waved to Kim (who was doing a primitive ballet along the paving), slipped into a stall and was almost in her suit when she heard the child scream; not a pretend-delighted-to-be-terrified squeal, but one of real dread.

IV

Caitlyn floated face down, long hair fanned out like a sea plant, skin a cold perfect white. After a paralyzed moment, Erica dove into the pool, and quick strokes brought her to the body, which she towed to the poolside.

"Run, have them call a doctor! Send the gardeners over!" She shouted to Kim, who broke off wailing and streaked away.

Caitlyn was dead weight. Erica couldn't heave her up on the side, but the two tanned, husky men who had been working in the roses ran up. Quickly, they raised Caitlyn's limp flame-bikini-clad body and stretched her on the paving.

"She's not breathing," one stated.

Erica turned her over and knelt, applying her mouth to Caitlyn's slack one, forcing air into the other's lungs, continuing the slow deep respiration till her vision blurred and lights flashed in her brain.

"I'll take over," said a deep voice.

Strong hands eased her aside. Gulping for breath, Erica watched Angier hold Caitlyn's head and resume the kiss of life. Almost immediately, stricken with something alarmingly close to envy, Erica turned away.

Hadn't Angier often held Caitlyn like this, in love, his breath mingled with hers for pleasure? Even unconscious and near death, the woman had a melting fullness that promised delight, a body that knew and wantonly enjoyed love. And as she stirred, her first instinctive movement was toward Angier.

He drew back and got to his feet, face tight in a lack of expression that itself became eloquent.

"Again?" he said wearily.

She pushed herself up. At a nod and a word from Angier the gardeners moved off, glancing appreciatively and curiously backwards.

"Angier! You think I—tried to drown myself? It's not true!" She looked down at her feet, wrinkling her brow as if puzzled and trying to remember, and said in a tone of mounting fright, "I didn't put on this suit! I was just sunning there on the lounge, in my regular clothes!" She caught his hands, shook him. "Angier, someone tried to kill me! Someone dressed me in my swimsuit and left me to drown!"

"Really, Caitlyn!" Angier's voice was frigid. He almost flung her hands off him. "It's too lame a story even for you! At least your poison false alarm and the gas jetting out were credible—till it developed that you had staged both. But this story—"

Checking himself, he took her wrists. Pleading entered his tone. "You almost finished yourself this time, Caitlyn! Too many knockout drops. If Miss Hastings hadn't known the mouth-to-mouth process, you'd be past it all. Please, while there's time, let me take you to a doctor!"

"A head-shrinker?" Caitlyn shrilled. "I don't want any vile-minded psychiatrist tampering with my mind, ruining my talent!"

"Caitlyn," he said wearily, "you've got so far out that you're not going to have any career if you can't regain your balance!"

Her wide green eyes blazed, then misted. "All I need is for you to—to care, Angier—"

In desperation, he thrust her claiming arms away. His jaw was hard under taut skin. "Caitlyn, no one can change what time does to us. If you won't help yourself, at least stop these theatrics! The next time you do something foolish, you're leaving Lady Gift."

"I'll go gladly the moment you've finished my play—our play, Angier!" She rose shakily, her slender body a voluptuous plea as she held out her arms. "Our fates are tied! You know it, even if you won't admit it! Only the plays I've starred in have ever made you fame or money!"

"They just happened to be the best plays!" Angier sucked in his breath. "How can I work with you attempting suicide, throwing tantrums, quarreling with Sybil and the staff? My God, Caitlyn, I never married you! I owe you nothing! This has to stop!"

She put her face into her hands and began to cry.

Angier swore and turned on his heel, noticing Erica, an unwilling eavesdropper, who was holding Kim at the end of the patio.

"Think this is good listening for your charge?" he asked witheringly, checked himself and forced a laugh. "Sorry, Miss Hastings! You did a good job; but don't expect any thanks from that vixen!"

"I didn't help her for thanks," said Erica. "Come along, Kim, let's have that swim."

As they passed Caitlyn, the woman shivered and said somberly, "You believe him. But as God judges, I did not pretend! Before I have, but not this time!"

Erica sent Kim on into the pool, spoke beneath the splashing. "But that would mean someone tried to kill you!"

43

"Yes."

"If you really think so, why don't you call the police?"

"They would talk to Angier, to everyone, and agree I was lying." Caitlyn tried to smile, but her eyes, Erica thought, held a growing terror mingled with grief. "Anyway, Miss Hastings, it may be I would rather die than expose my killer. Thank you for—for saving me this time." She went into the dressing room. A few minutes later, from the pool, Erica saw her come out dressed.

She must think Angier had tried to kill her; or else she had tried to kill herself and now was disavowing the attempt.

Surely that was it, Erica decided firmly, taking Kim by leg and arm and swirling her around in the water till she squealed in glee. Caitlyn admitted to earlier fake suicide attempts and was clearly almost always on the verge of hysteria. Besides, Angier Matthews did not strike Erica as a murderer, at least not as a man who would drug a sleeping woman and throw her in the pool to drown. He might—anyone might—get angry enough for violence that could conceivably kill, but overbearing and arrogant as he was, Erica got from him no impression of a capacity for premeditated evil.

She raced Kim up and down the pool several times, and, discovering that the child didn't know how to float, began to teach her how, at first supporting the back of Kim's head till rigidity left the neck muscles and the girl began to trust the water, believe it would hold her up.

They were leaving the pool, Kim in high spirits and apparently not troubled by the near drowning of Caitlyn, when Angier came out of the men's dressing room. His black trunks exposed a powerful, heavy, yet not ungraceful body, fit as only regular exercise could keep it once a man was in his forties.

Did he look a bit disappointed to see them going? He gave a strand of his daughter's dripping hair an awkward tweak, as if he didn't do it often.

"Seems that you're going to have a good holiday then, Kimberley?"

"Oh, yes, thanks, Angier!" Kim clasped Erica with embarrassing fervor. "I can float on my back! I just learned how!"

"Well done!" he chuckled. But his grey eyes rested on the beautiful child with an expression almost of torment. Did she remind him of her mother? Taking a sudden long breath, he smiled over Kim's head to Erica.

"Well done!" he said again, and he didn't mean simply teaching Kim to float. He took his daughter's arm.

"Come show me the float," he urged.

Kim's eyes glistened. "Dee-lighted!"

In seconds, she was letting the water buoy her up, blinking happily past water drops on her nose at Angier, who watched with Erica from the paving.

"Excellent!" he said. "I've been trying to teach you that for years. This demands a celebration. May I take you ladies to dinner tonight?"

"Me?" sputtered Kim, jackknifing in her excitement.

"Both of you," said Angier and glanced at Erica, his eyes so happy and intent that she felt a shock run through her and looked away in confusion as she felt blood mount to her face.

She mustn't be a fool! Angier was grateful for her discovery of Caitlyn and the knack she seemed

45

—hopefully!—to possess of managing his exuberant yet disturbingly solitary daughter.

"That would be very nice," said Erica, forcing her tone to be pleasant but not eager. "When should we be ready?"

"Seven's early enough." Had her manner dampened him, or was he already regretting this inroad into his precious time? "There's a very good restaurant, an old coaching inn, near the cathedral. We can go there, stroll about the cathedral a bit if you'd enjoy that, and still be home by Kim's bedtime."

Kim splashed joyously. "Good! I'll show Erica the Lady's effigy!"

"You've got macabre tastes for a little girl," Angier observed. "If I catch Peg loading your head with that nonsense again—"

"Oh, she doesn't, Angier!" protested Kim, sobering with anxiety. "Truly, she doesn't! And I—we—that is, Erica and I don't believe in ghosts. Do we, Erica? Not till we see them or hear them!"

Angier gave a crisp nod. "I'm glad to hear that," he said, gaze flicking to Erica. He dove in, scooped up Kim, and deposited her, giggling and kicking, on the side of the pool. "Be ready at seven," he told them both, and submerged.

"I must be growing up," Kim remarked, as they changed in the dressing stalls warmed through the transparent plastic roof.

"Why?" asked Erica, starting guiltily. She had been pondering Angier, reliving that tingling, electric moment when their eyes met.

"Angier's never taken me to dinner just for fun—he has to, of course, when we're in London or on trips. And he—he just seems to like me better."

46

"Sometimes it's like that." Erica groped for an honest explanation. "Often people don't know how to talk to really young children, but once a child is old enough to understand things that interest them, they have no problem."

"Perhaps that's it." Living with adults had given Kim a quaint philosophical way of talking when she wasn't overcome with zest or woe. "Anyway, tonight we'll have a splendid dinner and visit the Lady's tomb!"

It was so obviously her idea of a magnificent outing that Erica lacked the heart to say she would prefer to settle in more before viewing any tomb of an alleged ghost. Hand in hand again, they drifted to the house.

In full light, the hall was even more imposing than it had been last night, but Erica looked away from the imploring fingers carved on the banister as she followed Kim up the stairs.

Kim went to do her lessons while Erica unpacked. Her simple, tailored clothes looked out of place in the elaborate, gold trimmed wardrobe, and her plain white underwear seemed forlorn when nested in the rose-satin-lined bureau drawers.

Her sense of apology mingling with assertion, she put her birch-handled hairbrush on the crystal-and-silver dressing table, and grimaced in humorous despair at her face in the triple mirror.

She was a wren in surroundings made for a bird of paradise! If only the splendor were tattered! Then she might reasonably have asked Angier Matthews to let her do it over.

But though it must have been decorated ten years ago, the room had no discoloration on the walls, no spot on the thick rose carpet nor mark on the furniture.

47

It looked like a room that had been asleep, and now, roused by one not its rightful mistress, it was determined to retain its cool perfection and atmosphere of frozen time.

Nonsense! Erica scolded herself. People had feelings about rooms, not rooms about people!

She had better just think of the room as an exceptionally elegant hotel accommodation. She would gradually acquire things to personalize it, temper the du Barry effect. Meanwhile, she could move the ivory-enameled writing desk near the window, where she could look out at the towering, dark green cedar of Lebanon with its layered boughs, and have a good view of the sundial in the rockery.

She quickly wrote to her mother, saying cheerful things about her work, though how much of it would reach that pitifully wandering mind was a painful doubt which Erica could not dwell on. Her mother, widowed young, and earning her living as a librarian, had always been subject to heavy depressions, which grew worse and longer-lasting as Erica grew older.

When Erica got her first job, she had urged her mother to stop working in the hope that more leisure would help. Mother was talented with ceramics and had long wanted time to develop her ideas. After twenty-five years, she said goodbye to the library and bought a kiln.

She did some lovely things: unicorns, one of which was the only ornament Erica had brought to England and which she would put on this writing desk; mermaids; mermen; griffins; centaurs; strange mythic beasts and half-humans. She did them in terra cotta and glazed them in white with aquamarine and golden touches. They had been taken by several boutiques and for a while a new life seemed to unfold for the quiet woman with the dreaming gentle eyes.

But the depressions had come again, blacker and longer, till Erica came home one evening to find her mother unconscious among the shards of her latest creations, an empty vial of sleeping pills in her hand.

She had taken so many that her stomach rejected them and she lived, but her doctor advised, and she agreed, that she needed help to go on living.

The private hospital, in spite of its arts program and extensive resources, seemed to provide only a comfortable swaddling, where the sick woman lapsed into dreams, some inner world; but at least the visions were not of horror now, and her therapist was hopeful.

"Personalities are self-healing to an often unappreciated degree," he said during Erica's final talk with him before deciding to vacation and research her Master's thesis in England and possibly find work there. "If we find your visits might help, we'll let you know, but my impression—and you must try not to be hurt by this—is that your absence might be a good thing for a while."

Erica looked at him in shock. "Why?" she asked angrily.

He put his hand over hers for a quieting moment. He was a solid, blond young man with a kind of bold masculine beauty like a carpenter angel.

"Miss Hastings, your mother has made you her life. In effect, she led a nun-like existence with little in the way of personal pleasure. It's possible that as you grew older, she grew more despondent about her vanished youth, and though she loves you, she could not help feeling jealous. A continual fight to suppress such normal resentments could tear such a sensitive, introverted person apart. It's not your fault and whatever you do, you must not develop guilt about her that will block your own life. Go to England, by all means, and if you do decide to stay, do it with my assurance that I think it may help your mother rather than hurt her."

She was leaving when he said quietly, "Miss Hastings?"

"Yes?"

"You do understand that there is nothing organic about this problem?" When she stared in surprise, he added bluntly, "Sometimes people are afraid such illnesses run in their family. I just wanted to assure you that your mother's trouble seems a completely personal, individual one."

"I must be stupid," said Erica, "but I'm so prosaic that the idea of any inherited sickness never occurred to me."

"Fine," smiled the doctor. "That confirms my opinion of your emotional balance. Be happy in England. By the time you come home, your mother may be well enough to leave the hospital."

After Erica sealed the letter, she took out a little figurine of a unicorn, a melancholy, humorous, plump creature, hooves crossed appealingly as it sat up on its haunches. One fat aquamarine tear squeezed from the left eye. She put it on the desk, and hoped fervently that before long her mother would be able to move from her inner prison into the real world, again creating her whimsical beings and fabulous creatures.

Erica glanced at her watch. Kim would be busy till lunch. There was time to do her last unpacking, the part she had put off as long as possible.

Slowly she opened the partially uncleared suitcase

that held books. She set the books between a pair of crystal swan bookends on the bureau. Most of them she had bought in London, source books for her thesis on the court masques written by Ben Jonson, with costumes, sets and stage machinery designed by the great architect Inigo Jones.

She had enjoyed teaching speech and dramatics in high school, but a Master's would let her look for work at college level where her students would be more ambitious and critical. She hadn't whispered to anyone, not even Martin, her secret longing to someday write a play, but it had something to do with her eager response to Angier's advertisement in the Sunday *Times: Playwright, country house eighty miles from London, requires American companion-tutor for nine-year-old girl.* He had tentatively hired her by phone after discussion of salary and qualifications.

And here she was. . . .

Beside the thesis books she put a few indispensables from home. Last of all, she added the one she had brought as a kind of emotional barometer to measure her recovery from Martin.

A teacher in the university night classes where she had gradually acquired most of the credits toward her Master's, Martin had at first joined his students for coffee in the Student Union cafeteria. He intrigued Erica at once with his good-humored weariness and knowledge. It seemed natural that he should start taking her home when he learned that otherwise she had to catch a bus. They began leaving the others earlier, stopping at a tavern for wine or a sandwich.

She knew she was in love as she had never been before. Though all she could think about, when her attention wasn't specifically engaged, was Martin, with his thick sandy hair and quizzical eyes, she was happy to let the feeling deepen, refusing to think of marriage or anything beyond the present moment.

One night, though they had never more than kissed good-night, he suggested they visit a motel.

"I'm not a prude," said Erica, concealing a twinge of shock. "But I don't think we're ready for that yet."

Martin stared at her a long, heart-stopping moment. Then he drove her home, didn't speak till she was getting out of the car. "It's past time I leveled with you, Erica. If by ready, you mean able to marry, then we never will be."

Frozen, she gazed at him. He went on in a rush of self-disgust and pleading. "Erica, please—don't think I'm the professorial wolf who victimizes students! I've never acted this way before, never felt like this! But I *am* married. I have two children. In a very deep way, I do love my wife."

"Then—then—"

"You've been enchantment, Erica, right from the start." He bowed his head, gripping the wheel as if to keep himself from touching her. "You're always in my mind. But I know myself. If I left my wife and children for you, the dream would turn into a nightmare. With an affair, we could be happy while we were, and when we weren't, we could let it go."

"What made you think I'd be happy with an affair?" she asked in a tone so dead and controlled she marveled at it herself.

He shook his head. "I didn't—think. I suppose I just hoped. Lots of girls these days aren't especially interested in marriage. You're so self-reliant and capable that—"

That I've been imagining having a son with eyes and a mouth like yours.

"One thing you've got to believe," he said into her numbed silence. "I love you." He made a rough gesture of despair. "I know I should have told you I was married, but at first it didn't seem to matter, and by the time I knew I should, I just kept putting it off."

"Well, it's no tragedy," she managed to say at last, trying to laugh. "Certainly I wouldn't try to ruin a marriage. I—I hope you go on being in love with your wife." Her voice slipped out of control. "I just would suggest that before you give other women lifts home, you tell them you're securely taken."

"Dammit, I don't intend to take anyone else home!" They were in front of her apartment. He jumped out and walked her to the door, kissed her once, long and angrily, and turned away.

She started catching the bus right after night class, thanking heaven the semester was nearly over. For a week, he followed her cue and was politely formal, but the night of their last session, he was waiting by the bus stop.

"Let me take you home, Erica." He laughed with unhappy self-mockery. "After tonight, you can forget you ever knew me!"

They stopped for wine at the funny little tavern where they had first held hands, where she had first been sure he cared about her.

"Erica," he said with a wistful humility that reached through her numbed sense of unreality to hurt her. "I'm not going to lay snares or pester you. Just promise me something?"

"What?"

"I don't have anything new to offer, so it's a nerve to even ask. Still, I can't help it." His eyes held hers, as they had so often. "Erica, if you decide sometime —anytime, for this won't happen to me again—that you want us to have what we can, you will tell me, won't you? I'm not going to ask you again, or be a bother. But I need to believe that if you ever change your mind, you'll let me know."

She finished her wine and stood up. "I don't want to change my mind, Martin. But if I do, I'll tell you. Now—please take me home!"

During the next week, her mother entered the hospital, and with all the work done toward her degree except the thesis, Erica had decided to go to England. She absolutely could not stay in the same town with Martin; not for a long time, maybe not ever.

And when she could read the book of Donne's poems that Martin had given her without longing for his voice or touch, then she would know she was cured.

> *I am two fools, I know,*
> *For loving, and for saying so . . .*

The luncheon bell rang. She had fallen into a fit of glooms! Hurriedly she brushed her hair, washed and went down the hall.

V

Angier was not at the table but the rest of the household were, Kim startlingly so. Somehow she had contrived to pin her long shining hair up into a sort of lopsided sugar loaf. Pins stuck out from every angle and the whole was secured by twine only partially concealed by a flaming cerise ribbon.

"Most impressive, Kimberley," said Malcolm, rising to seat Erica, and giving her an appreciative look. "Is it the latest style from America?"

Kim cast a demure glance, tinged with pleading, at Erica. "I think it helps me look—dis-distinguished!"

"Extinguished," snapped Caitlyn. She looked marvelous in a white knit tunic, but her fright of the morning had not improved her temper. "Malcolm, will you, darling?" And she held out her glass.

"First, second and third courses, eh, Cait?" asked Malcolm jocularly. He filled her glass, topped up his and Sybil's, and started to pour into Erica's.

"No, thanks," she said quickly. It was a sparkling red wine, of the sort Martin had liked.

"Maybe she'd prefer a beer," suggested Sybil. Pleasant though the ex-wife secretary was, she had a patronizing edge to her manner that slightly annoyed Erica.

"Water's fine," she said, sipping at hers.

She selected slices of cold meat from a large platter,

55

added a cut of creamy Caerphilly cheese, crackers and tomatoes, and realized that she was hungry.

Strange about Angier. Was he really so busy he couldn't come to his table or didn't he like the people he had ranged about it?

Erica took a bite of meat, encountered Caitlyn's horrified green eyes, and stopped chewing.

"What's wrong?"

"You eat flesh—like all these others," Caitlyn accused. She had only salad and cheese on her plate. "Don't you know if you eat creatures now, they will eat you in another life?"

"Steady, Cait," soothed Malcolm. "You're mixing up Karma and the transmigration of souls." He spread his hands toward Erica. "If Cait had her way, we'd be crunching nut rissoles and soybeans!"

"Laugh and enjoy it," Caitlyn said darkly. "I tell you that the suffering of animals in tight feeding cages and abattoirs is covering the earth with a killing miasma—poisoning mankind, driving us to wars and to killing each other. Only imagine! In France, where they sell horsemeat, they hang up the poor beast's head!"

Sybil put down her fork. "Thanks very much, Caitlyn. Now you've put us all off our lunch, I hope you're content!"

"If you can't face the truth of what you're eating, should you have it?" triumphed Caitlyn. She smoothed her white suit close to her slender waist, glanced downward with satisfaction, and smiled at Sybil. "Anyway, darling, it won't hurt you to miss a meal."

"No one complains of your figure, dear!" shot back Sybil. "It's your kinky mind that breeds chaos!"

"Ladies!" interposed Malcolm with an indulgent

chuckle. He turned his sharply defined falcon's head toward Erica, the layered fall of his hair shifting at his neck like a bird's feathers. "Miss Hastings, we need to sort out how to handle your work permit so it will be approved by the Home Office as not depriving some worthy British subject of a job. I thought we might combine business and pleasure tonight at the village pub, which has very good food and is all the picturesque things one expects from a place called St. Peter's Beard."

"You can't get vegetables there," shuddered Caitlyn. "Only fish and meat."

"The best in Wessex!" agreed Malcolm.

"It sounds wonderful," Erica regretted. "But Kim and I are having dinner in town—"

"Angier's taking us to the old coaching inn just outside the Cathedral close!" broke in Kim.

All eyes swung to Erica, Sybil's with direct reappraisal, Malcolm's ruefully startled, and Caitlyn's glittering with resentment as she came to her feet, confronting Erica.

"Angier never takes me out! When we're at Lady Gift, it's always work, work, work—he doesn't even come to meals! Why should he take *you* to dinner?"

"Perhaps because he doesn't like to be upbraided over his roast beef as if he were a cannibal," Sybil slipped in deftly.

"It's a reward for me," defended Kim. "I learned to float, and Angier was proud! Wasn't he, Erica?"

"Floating! What's floating?" shouted Caitlyn.

Kim's lips trembled. Her brows rushed together, making her resemble Angier. "You're lucky you *did* float today. You'd have drowned if Erica hadn't helped you! Why should Angier take you out? He does all the time when you're in London or New York! You —you're just a great huge pig!"

"I'm not huge!" blazed Caitlyn.

Malcolm diverted her fury. "So you almost drowned, sweet Cait? How did that happen?"

Sybil looked at him significantly. "Can't you guess?" Turning to the actress, she chided, "Caitlyn, we know you're overstrained, but these fake suicides are a bore. Please see a specialist and get something to help you straighten out."

As if her bones had melted, Caitlyn sat down and wept. "It was not fake! I knew you'd both think so, that's why I didn't tell you! Someone did, really did, put my swimsuit on me and put me in the water!"

"Without waking you?" demanded Malcolm. "Oh, pack it in, Cait darling! You do need a doctor!"

"I was drugged!"

Sybil and Malcolm exchanged glances and shrugged. Caitlyn whirled to Erica. "Do you believe as they do?" she demanded.

"I—I don't know what to think," Erica stammered. "But it never hurts to see a doctor when things get to be too much."

Caitlyn shot her a gaze of pure hatred, swept from the room and slammed the door so the china and silver rattled.

"Another gracious meal at Lady Gift," Malcolm said. "Since you're taken tonight, how about tomorrow?"

Erica hesitated. She rather liked this cool, intelligent man, but his good-naturedly callous treatment of Caitlyn put her off a bit, though the actress was certainly hard to like. Still, because of the way lives at Lady Gift were intermeshed, it was surely best to

58

understand each person as much as possible. And Malcolm might tell her more about Angier; perhaps he knew what had happened to Kim's mother.

"Let me see if I can arrange something for Kim," Erica said.

"Oh, Peg will stay with her," Malcolm laughed. "Before you came, Peg had a cot outside Kim's room and she's as watchful of her as a mother bear of its cub! Have you met her?"

"Not yet."

"Better seek her out before she feels slighted." Malcolm smiled as he sipped his wine. "I'll wager she's had several good looks at you from the windows and around corners." He rose as Erica did, and bowed. "I'll hope to show you St. Peter's Beard tomorrow night then!"

"If I can fix it, that'll be lovely," Erica said. She nodded a goodbye to Sybil, who responded through a lazy swirl of smoke, and went along the gallery with Kim beside her.

"What will we do now, Erica?" asked Kim. "I haven't shown you the house yet. Or we could find Peg, or walk to the village, or—"

Erica had noticed that Kim's elbows had a ground-in grubby look, and the fantastically dressed hair needed a shampoo.

"I would like you to introduce me to Peg, and if there's time, it would be fun to see the house. But if your father's taking us out, we both need to look as nice as we can. I need to shower and wash my hair. So do you."

Kim grasped her topknot protectively. "Oh, no!" she wailed. "I wanted to wear my hair like this!"

"We can do it up again," promised Erica. "I've got

some lovely shampoo that highlights your natural color, and I think I've got a rhinestone crescent hair clip that would really set off that style!"

Half an hour later, Erica helped Kim to step out of the huge, old oval tub that stood on bronze-clawed legs in a large bathroom built on two levels, dressing room above the bath and mirrored lavatory, while the stool like the one in Erica's bath, was shut off from sight by shoulder-high tiled wall.

"You didn't pull my hair so much as Peg does," said Kim, face emerging from the towel with which Erica was vigorously drying the long shining tresses. "You aren't going to put it up on curlers, are you?"

"No, we'll just brush out the tangles and you can dry while you show me the house and help me find Peg."

"We can go to the sun roof first," Kim decided, skinning headlong into shorts and sleeveless pullover that were too tight for her beautifully proportioned compact little body.

From the bath, they passed through Kim's room with its incongruous mixture of shabby child's things and cast-off adult relics. Though Kim's usual voice was a subdued, soft scream of excitement, she put her finger to her lips in a shh! and tiptoed past Angier's door down the gallery.

"This wing is Angier's," Kim said. "First there's his study, then a bedroom and bath, and he has a little kitchen and bar tucked in by his bedroom." She sighed. "That way, when he's having a tremendous good patch of work, he doesn't have to come out at all."

She opened a door off the gallery into a small passage which was empty except for a plain ladder that ran upwards into darkness. Kim started up it, lithe as a monkey. Erica hung back.

"Isn't there a light?"

Kim swallowed a scornful sound and switched on a light that glowed dimly yellow from above. Erica climbed after her, stepped out into an attic on a catwalk that appeared to follow the gallery below, solid planking down the center of the unfloored ceilings. The roof slanted to within four feet of the floor.

"You can go all the way around the house on this boardwalk," Kim explained. "But only part of the way is lit so you need a candle or electric torch to do it." She skipped a bit, proud to be leading an exploration. "The sun roof's right along here. Nobody knows about it except Peg and me. Look, you just duck through this window and come out above the well in the center of the house. The gallery runs around the well. Mind you don't bump your head!"

They were out on a sheltered, lower part of the roof, a flat portion with one long, broad chimney dividing it. Erica looked down into the well, a sort of paved courtyard enclosed by the four walls of the great house.

She jumped at a sudden cry from Kim. Nervous because of the height—it was sixty feet down to that paving and a fall would almost certainly kill or maim anyone who slipped—Erica spun, instinctively reaching for the child, who glared around the chimney.

"What are *you* doing up here?" Kim demanded in outrage.

Caitlyn, turning over and reaching for her sunglasses, pulled a towel over her nude body and snapped at Erica, "I trust one of your first priorities will be to teach this impudent girl how to treat guests! Since it's obviously unsafe for me to sunbathe by the pool, I had to find another place." She stretched and yawned. "This suits admirably!"

"But it's my place!" Kim's face had screwed up into a frustration that alarmed Erica. Brought up as she had been it was no wonder, but the child's emotions were altogether too extreme and violent. She badly needed equilibrium, some calming down. She clenched her small brown fists. Tears glinted on her long dark eyelashes. "Who told you about the roof?"

"My God, but you're tiresome!" Caitlyn sat up, quickly put on her underwear and tunic. "When Angier marries me, I'll cure you of that fast enough!"

"He's not going to marry you," retorted Kim, and with a coolness Erica had to admire though she deplored it, Kim continued, "Tell me how you knew about this place, or I'll tell Angier you swore at me. I heard him tell you he'd send you packing next time you did!"

"Hellbrat! Eavesdropper!"

"Who told you?" Kim persisted.

"Your precious Peggie did!"

Kim recoiled, hand going to her mouth. "No! Peg wouldn't! This is *our* place—"

"You lost no time bringing your keeper up!" sniffed Caitlyn. "Well, I intend to sunbathe, but we may as well have an agreement. I'll only come for a few hours after lunch. The rest of the time, it's yours!"

"I don't want you up here anytime!" cried Kim.

Erica put a hand to her shoulder, but Kim pulled free, face contorted. "Angier's got his wing and no one goes there! You grown-ups have your own rooms and the lounges and library and dining rooms and the run of the grounds! Can't I have one place to myself?"

"You called me a big pig at lunch," remarked Caitlyn, going through the window and giving Kim a tight little smile. "Well, you are a small pig! I wish you luck with her, Miss Hastings. You'll need it!"

Unbelievably, she stuck out a pointed pink tongue at Kim and disappeared. Erica fought back appalled laughter, lost any urge to smile when she saw Kim's face set in a most unchildlike concentration of fury.

"I hate her!" the girl cried passionately. "I hate her top to bottom and—and if she comes up here again, I hope she falls off."

"Kim!"

"I don't care! She's a crazy witch, Peg says. Angier ought to send her away!"

"There may be reasons why he thinks he shouldn't," Erica said, more briskly than she felt. "Anyway, it's a wonderful sunning place. May I come up sometimes?"

"Of course!" Kim brightened, restored as a bestower of favors. "Would you like to stay awhile now?"

"It would be nice, but I really must meet Peg."

"And I'll show you the rest of the house!"

They went back along the catwalk in what was almost darkness after the sunlight of the roof. The ladder, unsecured at the top, wobbled as they went down. Erica made a mental note to ask for some wire to fasten it to the nearby beams.

Back in the gallery outside the ladder closet, Kim led the way they had come, and turned into a spacious room with two windowed alcoves, each with a love seat and several armchairs. A corniced fireplace dominated the room, the picture above it looking like a late Constable, landscape transfigured with light and shadow. The huge *bergere* suite, upholstered in wine velvet, centered around a table whose top was a bronze elliptical map set in brown leather, with brass signs of the zodiac running around the edge.

Carpet and draperies were a green so dark they

looked black. Antique tables, chests and cabinets had a mellow patina that spoke of much polishing. In its richly somber way, the room was beautiful, but in spite of eight large windows, it had a quality of darkness. The many pictures were in muted or deep tones, and the statuettes, one for each of the twelve labors of Hercules, were in bronze. Even the books scattered about the tables and chests were tooled in deep green and brown leathers.

What a difference color could make in this room! Erica pictured an arrangement of peonies or yellow roses on the table behind the long *bergere* settee.

A small bar, sherry and glasses set out on a tray, was in a recess on one side of the fireplace. On the other was a record-player-television built into a carved cabinet with sliding doors.

"I don't come in here often," said Kim. "And when I do, I sit over there in the alcove where I can feel the sun."

They turned into a large formal dining room next. A sideboard ran the length of one wall. A built-in oak chest stretched beneath six windows that looked out on the Douglas fir. Candelabra gleamed from the Regency table flanked by high-backed chairs upholstered in tapestry, and a matching wall hanging of a medieval hunt decked one wall.

"Once in a while Angier gives a party for his business friends," Kim said. "That's the only time this room is used."

Next came the small dining room where Erica had already been through two peculiar meals. Continuing in the gallery past two doors, Kim said, "That's Mrs. Shell's kitchen and pantry. The kitchens used to be downstairs, but Peg says that was when they had six scullery maids, a butler and two cooks. Besides Mrs. Shell and Peg, we just have two daily women from the village who do most of the heavy cleaning." She opened two other doors, let Erica take a quick peek. "This is the sewing room and Peg used the other when she used to sleep by my room!"

They had circled the gallery and come to the banister of carved hands. In the central hall, beneath the skylight, they paused. "Malcolm, Sybil, and Caitlyn have rooms down here," Kim told Erica. "And there's another lounge, the sun room. It's really sort of theirs, so I won't take you there. But here's the library!"

It was the largest room of all, shelved from floor to ceiling except for window bays and the huge marble fireplace. Persian carpets with intricate jewel-hued patterns glowed on the polished floor. Easy chairs were placed near windows or lamps, a record player was littered with albums of the Beatles, Simon and Garfunkel and Peter, Paul and Mary. There was a big desk, a typewriter on a rolling stand, a tremendous magazine rack, and two old refectory tables which held large art books and an unabridged dictionary.

"Don't you just love it?" asked Kim, stretching out her arms to encompass the room. "It's my favorite place in the grown-ups' house. I can play records and read, and the books are like company, all waiting politely to get to know you when you read them."

Erica had already spied several books she had been wanting to read. She might even find thesis material here. "It's a wonderful library!" she said.

Kim nodded. "If I could eat my ice-lollies here, it would be absolutely perfect!"

"Ice-lollies, books and the Beatles would be too much luxury!" Erica teased. "But what do you mean by the grown-ups' house?"

Kim lowered her voice as they crossed the hall to a bare little room apparently used to store cleaning materials and equipment. "I mean where the grown-ups go. But the servants and I know other parts, like the roof and down here." She opened a trap door, flicked a switch, and started down.

"It's time I met Peg," protested Erica.

"This is the quickest way." Kim's voice had a sepulchral ring.

Shrugging, Erica followed. To her surprise, the cellar was warm. As they went along the passage, a roaring sound got louder.

"It's the central heating," explained Kim. "It stays on part of the time even in the summer to heat water." As they walked, she turned light switches off and on.

They passed the immense heater with its glaring red eyes, turned into a big room with a center drain, sinks, old-fashioned boilers, and a modern washing machine and drier.

"You can guess what this is," grinned Kim. The next room was used for storage. "Now for the wine cellar," Kim directed. "It's a teensy light here."

They stepped out of the cool room with its dimly gleaming racked bottles. Kim shut the door. "Now we're out from under the grown-ups' house!" she breathed. "We've come all the way under the courtyard well and we go up these stairs into what used to be the butler's pantry."

They entered a sizable room floored with linoleum. A table and several chairs stood near the window. There was a cupboard with a few dishes and staples, an electric kettle, a stove and a small refrigerator.

"This is where the gardeners have their afternoon and morning tea," said Kim. She looked wistfully at a calico cat sunning on the chintz-covered window seat, could not resist giving it a pat, but washed her hand in the small sink at once. "That's to get rid of the dander so I won't get wheezy," she said matter-of-factly. "Lorna Doone is Peg's cat. Isn't she a darling?"

"Very nice," said Erica, who admired cats without liking them much.

"Peg ought to be around here someplace," frowned Kim. "Maybe she's in the game larder. That's where they used to clean hares and deer and fowl and hang them till they were cooked. We still clean fish and chickens there, but mostly it's used for making flower arrangements."

They passed through a hall that led to what Kim named as the tradesmen's entrance.

"Peg!" called Kim. "Peg, are you there?" She opened a heavy hinged door and pushed through it, pulling Erica after her.

VI

There was a scuffling and flurry of movement. The
youngest of the gardeners who had helped pull Caitlyn
from the pool, a sunburned man with yellow hair and
blue eyes, mumbled something and ducked past, to
leave Erica watching a dark-eyed, plump young
woman with clear, very fair skin, highly colored at the
moment with blushes. She had a full, almost flaunting
body, and as she recovered from her first confusion,
she faced Erica with bold assurance, and held out her
arms to Kim, who ran to be enfolded.

There was something touching in the way the big
country girl possessively held the thin, finely made
child. *A bear with her cub*, Malcolm had said.

"Where've you been all the day, poppet?" she asked,
with an accent that sounded to Erica as if she were
talking with a mouthful of hot potatoes. "I've missed
you, I have!" And she shot an accusing glance at Erica.

Kim wriggled loose. "I've been doing lessons and
showing Erica—oh, Erica! This is Peg! Peg, I've been
taking Erica around Lady Gift. *Why* did you tell that
mean old Caitlyn about the sun roof? She was up there,
just as though it was hers!"

Peg rumpled Kim's hair, observing Erica sharply
from the corner of her eye. "She asked me where there

was a quiet safe place she could sunbathe, poppet, and what else could I be telling her?" Peg tapped her head meaningfully. "The poor woman thinks someone tried to drown her!"

"She's probably just putting on," grumbled Kim.

"Another minute in the water and I doubt we could have saved her," cut in Erica. "I have no idea how she got in the pool, but she did nearly drown."

Peg shook her head, half-laughing, half-exasperated. "She's a rare, mad, wild one, that!" With an air of grasping the nettle, she looked straight and direct at Erica for the first time. "How do you think you'll like Lady Gift?"

"It's very beautiful."

"Now that's not saying how you like it, is it?" scored Peg. "It's not the jolly easiest place in the world to fit into." She added with relish, eyeing Erica speculatively, "You're not the first lady Mr. Matthews has found for Kim!"

"She's the prettiest!" Kim defended, circling Erica's waist in a swift hug.

Peg put a plump hand on the child's shoulder. "Pretty or plain, the others couldn't stick it long! It's always been Peg wound up sleeping by your door again." She gave Kim a little spank. "Run into the courtyard, poppet, and peek in the fig tree. Careful now!"

"What is it, Peg?"

"Go find out!"

Kim ran off. Peg drew Erica into a corner by the oversized sink over which meat hooks still dangled, and spoke in an undertone, "Miss Erica, you're a pretty lady—nice, too, I'll be bound! But please—don't let Kimmy get all fond of you too fast!"

69

"Why, Peggie, what do you mean?"

"You may decide not to stay on here. If you do go after a few weeks or months, I don't want to watch Kimmy eat her heart out after you!" Peg touched Erica's arm in a pleading command. "It's just a position to you, Miss! But it's the poppet's heart I'm thinking on!"

"I'm fond of Kim," said Erica.

"Fond!"

"Yes, indeed. I wouldn't pretend to love her after a day. But I can and do feel for her, Peggie." Erica gave the girl a direct, steady look. "I've taken the job. I think I can be good for Kim. You may be sure I'll stay unless something most unexpected comes up."

A sly look crossed Peg's face. Her laugh was a bit unpleasant. "Unexpected things do come up at Lady Gift, Miss!"

"So do they anywhere." Erica watched Peg and thought it best to speak frankly. "Peg, I have some idea of what Kim means to you and what you are to her. I've no wish to change any of that. But I am responsible for her. It will be much happier for all of us, especially Kim, if you and I can work together."

"Yes, Miss." Peg's tone was meek enough but her bold eyes were appraising, as if she wondered how long this new one would last.

Erica smiled. "I'm glad we've had this chance to talk. Could you stay with Kim tomorrow evening? Mr. Matthews said I should arrange my time off so that you or Mrs. Shell could be with Kim."

"Of course I'll stay with my lamb," said Peg. She winked broadly, tilting her broad, rather pretty face. "I like the lads, but it's off with them all if my poppet needs me."

"Have you been at Lady Gift long?"

"Four years now, starting when I was fifteen." The big dark eyes gave Erica a searching, almost challenging stare. "During that time, Kimmy's had a dozen nannies or governesses. They never lasted long."

"I wonder if I will?" laughed Erica. "So I can depend on you to take Kim in hand right after she's had dinner tomorrow?"

"To be sure!" Peg hesitated. "If you're going to be late, maybe I ought to put my cot outside her door," she suggested hopefully.

"I won't be that late," said Erica. She was sorry for the worshipping Peg, but troubled. Such fierce protectiveness made a good human watchdog, but, unchecked, what could it do to both Kim and the girl? "This is a sort of business dinner with Mr. Harrow."

Peg's mouth turned down. "That one?" she steamed. "Watch out for him! He's always carrying tales to Mr. Matthews, trying to get him to sell off Lady Gift as too much trouble and go live in America! He won't really want you to manage—and I've already heard Mr. Matthews tell him if you can't cope, he'll give up on this place."

Was there no end to the suspicion and deviousness at Lady Gift? The last thing Erica wanted to encourage was below-stairs gossip.

"Mr. Harrow seems most helpful and pleasant," she said.

Peg hunched a shoulder as if saying she had warned her, just as Kim came scudding in. "Oh, what lovely little birds!" she cried. "The mama was feeding them worms and their beaks opened so wide they seemed not to have anything else to their heads!"

"Mind you don't touch them," Peg cautioned.

"They're almost big enough to fly, and if you keep a good watch, you can see how they learn. Am I taking you swimming this afternoon?"

"Erica took me this morning," Kim said.

Peg's face fell. "She could go again," Erica felt compelled to say almost apologetically. "But I promised to do her hair up in a new style for going out tonight, and if it gets wet, there won't be time."

"Never mind," said Peg, giving Kim a squeeze. "I'll be up after dinner tomorrow, poppet, and we'll have a fine natter and story-telling before you go to bed!"

Ghost stories? wondered Erica as she followed Kim upstairs. But it didn't seem the time to quell Peg more than necessary.

The stair passage led to a door that opened into Mrs. Shell's pantry. "This is the way the servants used to bring up all the food from the kitchens downstairs," explained Kim. "Don't you know it was an awful nuisance, trying not to trip with a suckling pig or pheasant on a platter? Peg's grandmother was one of the maids back then and she thinks it's a scandal to have the kitchen upstairs."

"She probably thinks Peg's mini-skirt is a scandal, too," Erica said wryly. "Times do change!"

Steering Kim into her own room and seating her at the triple mirror, Erica hunted up the rhinestone crescent, brushed the long chestnut hair till it gleamed, and experimented, under Kim's critical, multi-imaged gaze, till she got the hair swirled upward from the nape into a high diadem, securely pinned and set off with the crescent.

"It's scrumptious!" exulted Kim, arching her neck and eyeing herself in each of the mirrors in turn. "Will you help me pick out a dress that will match?"

That was hard to do, out of the bewildering closetful of grey school uniforms and a few outgrown dresses, blouses and skirts. "Sybil took me shopping last summer holiday," said Kim. "During terms, I don't need much besides the uni—ugly thing, isn't it, but I do like the mac and beret, they look sort of dashing, like what a spy might have." She tugged out various skirts, scanning them with growing anxiety. "Goodness me! I don't have *anything* to wear!"

She had better reason than most for that eternal feminine wail. Erica spotted a handsome but plainly short aqua sheath, inspected the hem.

Three inches. Holding it against a tearful, but suddenly hopeful Kim, Erica said, "This will work, and I've a silver coin link belt that will dress it up."

"Eric!" shouted Kim, dropping the *a*. "You're wonderful!"

"I hope you'll think so when I tell you none of those shoes can be worn till they're polished." The tumbled array of sandals, boots and plimsolls in the bottom of the wardrobe was indeed a scruffy sight.

"Drat!" scowled Kim. Dropping to her knees, she scavenged out a pair of strap sandals. "Well, I'll give them to Peg to clean."

"I've some brown polish in my room," said Erica. "Come along. You do the shoes while I fix your dress."

"But Peg's supposed to shine my shoes!"

"If Mohammed could clean his, you can do yours," Erica said firmly.

Kim jutted out a lower lip, but was soon sitting on a newspaper, polishing with all her might, while Erica lengthened the dress. Kim showed her an ironing board that was always left out in the sewing room, and the old hem pressed out without a trace.

Soon Kim looked like a small Artemis in the straight aqua shift with its silver belt and her high-piled hair. She begged leave to read on the chaise longue while Erica got ready, and was then caught between absorption in the fate of Anne Boleyn and interest in what Erica was doing. There was a companionable feeling about having the child there, strange to Erica but welcome. She had never been able to relax with her mother.

"You don't take very long to make up," Kim said with a touch of disappointment. "Once Caitlyn let me watch her, and it took an hour and a half! She put on false eyelashes, and all kinds of things!"

A touch of eye shadow, lipstick, and a flirt of powder, applied in five minutes, usually made Erica look as pretty as fussing for half an hour with foundations and such could. Tonight she had added what was for her the ultimate enhancement, mascara, which darkened her lashes to a satisfyingly dramatic shade. She didn't use it often; somehow she nearly always wound up with it blurred on her lower lids in a "hung-over" effect.

"Caitlyn knows how to use make-up," Erica told Kim. "I don't, so I quit before I make a hash of it."

"Angier doesn't like her make-up," Kim reported. "He told her once to save it for the stage."

"You shouldn't pass on such stories."

"It's true!" Kim insisted. "I swear it is!"

"So are lots of things." Erica worked her toes into her sheerest tights while Kim ran over to zip up the back of her primrose yellow full-skirted organza dress,

74

one of the few unabashedly romantic things Erica had ever let herself buy. That had been in the spring when she had expected to wear it often for Martin. He had never seen it. And she couldn't bear to wear it, until now.

"Part of growing up," she continued to Kim, "is learning what to say to whom."

"Then I don't want to grow up! Who wants to think every time they say anything?"

"It's not that drastic! You just learn not to say certain kinds of things."

"That sounds hyper—hypo—hypercritical to me!"

"I think you mean hypocritical, Kim." Erica gave her a laughing spank. "I also think you know very well what I mean!"

"Oh, I guess I do," grudged Kim, but the glow came back when she saw herself in the mirror.

She preened while Erica put necessities in a dressy handbag and noticed with gratitude that her mascara seemed properly set on the upper lashes.

It was exactly seven. As she turned the door knob, an incisive tap came from the other side and she stepped through the door almost into Angier Matthews' pearl-buttoned breast.

"Punctual—and pretty!" he laughed, steadying her. His gaze lingered appreciatively, then switched to Kim who stood demurely behind Erica, except for the eyes so like Angier's, which tilted hopefully upwards.

"Well!" he exclaimed, bowing over her hand. "Who is this exquisite creature?"

"Oh, Angier!" cried Kim, between pleasure and scorn. "You know perfectly well it's me!"

"Never!" He examined her with a marveling

75

scrutiny that made her squeal with laughter. "You can't be Kimberley Matthews! Your fingernails are clean and trimmed! Your elbows aren't grubby! Your shoes are shined! No," he ruled firmly, shaking his head, "you aren't Kim! But you look so nice I'll sneak you off to dinner anyway!"

Maidendown was called a city only by grace of its beautiful twelfth-century cathedral, but it was a charming place of uneven red-tiled roofs, thatched cottages, sudden little bridges over a gentle river, and a square where an outdoor market was still held Tuesdays and Saturdays flanked by modern businesses in old buildings.

The cathedral close dominated one end of the town, the square Norman tower rising above the walls that enfolded a small world of spacious lawns, colleges, private schools, and a few dwellings located in old flint buildings that had once housed the Bishop and his household.

"My—*ugh!*—school is down at the far end," said Kim, who had been sitting upright and sparkling-eyed between Erica and her father on the front seat of the jade-green Jaguar. "Angier, I want to show Eric the effigy of Lady Margaret! May I? Will you come, too?"

"If you find your school so—*ugh!*—maybe I should send you to boarding school," he said a bit grimly, but as he parked outside the close gate with its gilded blazonry and statue of some saint, his gaze softened as it fell on his daughter's upturned face. "Yes, I'll walk to the cathedral with you. We're early."

A cobbled road led from the gate to the cathedral. As Kim danced down it ahead of them, Angier said wryly, "I don't know if there's a word for lovers of stately tombs, but if there is, Kim should be called it! Absolutely dotes on puzzling out dates and tracking down facts on the lives of people whose tombs she's seen! She drags me through Westminster Abbey every time we go to London—"

"I think it's fascinating that Queen Elizabeth and Bloody Mary share a tomb!" defended Kim, spinning back to them. "And I was glad King James the First put up a splendid one for his poor mother! The Scottish lion looks more like a poodle, Eric, but Mary Queen of Scots has a much grander place than Elizabeth. I think she deserves it since she lost her head and all!"

They stepped inside the vaulted cathedral with its grey stone walls lit by spills of light from the brilliant stained-glass windows. Memorial plaques, from medieval days to present times, ran about the walls. Inscribed stones or metal plates on the floor marked the names of those underneath. On either side of the pews facing toward the high altar ran a row of tombs. Effigies lay on raised stone slabs, knights in armor or chain mail with their swords.

"The lion some of them have at their feet means they were brave and generous," whispered Kim. "Dogs were shown with women to signify faithfulness and devotion."

"This knight has a dog," observed Erica, pausing to study the calm, proud features of a lord who had died in the twelfth century.

"He was a crusader," explained Kim. "Their dogs mean that they followed their cause like a dog follows his master. Can you read Latin, Eric?"

"Very little."

"Drat! We don't have it at school for another year, and I just long to know what all the inscriptions say!"

"Maybe we can do something about that," said Erica. She saw to her surprise that Angier had taken a seat and appeared deep in thought.

"He doesn't like Lady Margaret's tomb," murmured Kim. "Come on, it's in a chapel by the cloisters."

Turning before the choir stalls, they went past several small private chapels. Kim paused outside the last one by the great door opening onto the roofed walk that led around a square court with a fountain and several huge trees.

"Here's the Lady!" Kim said softly. "I've named my best sleeping doll for her!"

Erica gazed at the white tomb, skin prickling at the graceful alabaster hands that twined around the base, the hands of Lady Gift, the hands on the banister.

Lady Margaret's figure was of alabaster, the hands so cruelly severed from her restored to clasp lilies and roses on her breast. "I pretend she's my mother," Kim said suddenly, "because she's so pretty and because my own mother's buried in America—just ashes in an urn, Angier says. Do you think it's all right, Eric? To pretend?"

"Why not, if it doesn't make you sad?" Erica put her arm around Kim's shoulders, feeling that it *was* sad if this murdered alabaster lady was the nearest to a mother that Kim could believe in.

Angier seemed preoccupied as they walked to the coaching inn outside the close gate, but after a deferential waiter had shown them to a corner table, he threw off the mood, chose a wine that he and the waiter agreed would please Erica, and helped her order before raising a dark eyebrow at his child.

"What will you have, Kimberley?"

"Prawns?"

"Right!" He nodded to the waiter who looked incredulous. "And then what?"

"Scotch salmon?"

"Right! Vegetables?"

"Must I?"

He quirked the same eyebrow at Erica, his rather long-jawed face looking boyish and young. "Must she?"

"There ought to be something in this nice lot of vegetables," Erica said.

They settled on croquette potatoes and raw sliced carrots. Angier ordered his meal with dispatch and thoroughness while Erica looked around, delighting in the beamed ceilings, the big old fireplaces, Toby jugs and gleaming copper and pewter on shelves and cabinets.

"You seem to like it," Angier commented. "Is this your first time in England?"

She told him that it was. He continued to question her in such a genuinely interested manner that Erica found herself telling him a little about her mother, her teaching experiences in the Houston ghetto, and even about her thesis on masques.

"Well, Kim!" exclaimed Angier to the girl who was raptly enjoying her prawns in spite of their pink potato-sproutish appearance. "Perhaps I need Miss Hastings more than you do!"

Kim uttered such a pained cry that other diners looked around, Erica caught her hand soothingly, and Angier reddened. "Easy, Kim! Can't you tell when I'm joking?"

"You—you don't often joke!" Kim snuffled, peering

79

at him through blinked-back tears.

Angier bit his lip, shrugged and grinned. "Full marks for that one! But," he quizzed, leaning forward and watching the child intently, "has your Miss Eric really got so important to you in just one day?"

"She's the first upstairs person who really likes me!" shot back Kim. "I was just a—a position to the nannies and others!"

"A precarious one," said Angier. But he seemed relieved as he settled back and looked at Erica. "I'm afraid the nannies and several other companion-tutors didn't work out. That's why I hoped an American might do the trick. Kim's very conscious of her heritage from over the Atlantic."

What would he say if he knew about Kim's fantasy of Lady Margaret?

As if deliberately steering away from the personal, Angier set himself to talking about England in a way that showed his knowledge and love of it. Kim chimed in with her almost absurd grasp of history, especially the more bizarre and bloody events. She seemed to know the name and story of every murdered king or queen from Edmund the Martyr to Charles the First, and her mind teemed with forlorn, beautiful captives like the Pearl of Brittany and Lady Jane Grey.

Dinner had a relaxed family air, and Kim chattered all the way to Lady Gift, so that Erica didn't notice Angier's withdrawn silence till he pulled up in front of the main entrance. He handed them both out, unlocked the door and held it as Erica and Kim passed inside.

"Good night," he said. And that was all.

Erica turned in surprise, but the door was shutting in her face.

What had happened? Snatches of the evening flurried through her head, but she could not remember anything that could have put him off. Kim grasped her hand, tugged toward the stairs.

"Never mind, Eric. He's just got his old play turning in his mind. At least that's what he tells me it is when he gets quiet and funny." She patted her hair and the crescent as they moved along the gallery to her room. "My hair stayed up perfectly, didn't it?"

"Yes," said Erica, forcing herself to smile and respond. "But now it's time to take it down."

Long after Kim was in bed, Erica lay awake. Angier had been interested and friendly—often even amusing. More than once his grey eyes had touched her in a way that made Martin seem even further away than he was. But Angier's good-night had been curt, hostile.

Kim might be right, of course. Possibly when he began to think about a play his mind clicked off from everything and everyone, locking him away even if physically he had to stay among people.

But if he were so intent on his work, why hadn't he come up yet? Erica realized that she had unconsciously been waiting for his steps, the opening of his door just down the gallery. She raised her head to peer at the luminous-handed clock.

Past midnight. Kim had been in bed well over an hour. Pulling the sheet up to her chin and turning over, Erica told herself that Angier must have come up while she was brushing her teeth or doing something to obscure the sound.

What had turned him strange? It had been such a lovely evening! But then he had gone silent, withdrawn. Erica turned over again.

He was exasperating, unfathomable! But if he thought she would be pleasant company at his beck and then would accept almost curt dismissal, he had things to learn about her, too!

Not that he would care. . . .

VII

After a breakfast of eggs and sausage next morning with little talk but much sidelong observation of her by Sybil and Caitlyn, Erica took Kim off to lessons in the library.

While Kim alternately chewed a pen and scratched at her paper (which she had decided to do on Katherine Parr, the wife who survived Henry the Eighth), Erica made multiplication-table flash cards. A quick test with them showed that math was math and Kim was Kim and seldom the twain did meet, but after a half hour's practice, Kim had at least stopped automatically saying, "Forty-nine!" for the answer to everything between six times six and nine times nine.

She also showed signs of flagging, so Erica put up the cards and moved on to stories from history.

After lunch—again a quiet, measure-taking meal except for Malcolm's reminder of their dinner engagement and a harangue from Caitlyn about the evil vibrations set up by the misery of feeder lambs who never set hoof to grass in their short, consumer-bound lives—Erica went through Kim's clothes, had the child try on doubtfuls, and decided that a shopping tour had priority tomorrow.

"Can I go swimming with Peg?" Kim asked, wriggling out of a pair of shorts and adding them to the pile accumulated for Oxfam.

"Is she expecting you?"

"Oh, yes! She's off between two and six and except for market days when she goes to town, we always do something. I'll just run down to her flat in the Clock House, shall I?"

In one way it seemed ridiculous to shadow a nine-year-old around her home grounds, but Erica preferred to be overcautious till she understood a lot more about Lady Gift and its denizens. She didn't want to make Kim nervous, though.

"I'll walk along with you," Erica said, "and then I'll stroll down through the Old Orchard."

"Mind the nettles," Kim warned.

"I'll put on rain boots and slacks," promised Erica. "See you in a minute!"

Quickly slipping into clothes she hoped would fend off the nettles, Erica thrust gloves and a pair of scissors into the pocket of her short jacket, and set off with Kim.

Beyond the mellowed bricks of the walled garden, Erica paused to scan the orchard. Its strangled, dying trees haunted her. She pulled on her gloves, took the scissors and grasped the ivy on the nearest tree, yanking off as much of it as she could, then scissoring at the tenacious remnants.

It was quixotic to think of freeing the trees with her scissors and a few snatched hours, but the tortured limbs seemed to beg for help, like the hands along the banister.

There was nothing she could give the dead Lady Margaret, but she might bring life back to at least some of these once fruitful trees.

It was a lowering, thunderstorm sort of day, sultry enough to make Erica shed her jacket after ten minutes of fierce battle with the ivy. Thunder rumbled. A few raindrops splattered her nose. She paused to look for the nearest shelter in case of a downpour.

The summer pavilion was at the far end of the orchard, two city blocks distant, but several sheds, all in poor repair but with apparently sound tile roofs, were built against the outside of the garden wall. She could try the nearest if a deluge came.

The tree Erica was working on had small green knobby fruits and as she ripped off the last of the smothering ivy, she wondered if it was too late to improve this season's apples. And would the bumps and maimed swellings diminish as the tree could breathe and drink again, or had it been cramped and pinioned so long that the distortions had become its unchangeable character?

She flexed her fingers, worked her tired shoulders back and forth, and attacked the next tangle of insidious green creepers.

An hour's steady work cleared three trees, exhausted Erica, and convinced her that scissors were no proper tool for ivy clearing. Rather than bother the gardeners for some kind of ripping implement, she'd buy one when she and Kim went shopping.

Hot and itching, she waved to Peg and Kim who were still in the pool, and went up to the house to shower.

Kim, standing a bit wistfully in front of Peg's bulk, waved goodbye to Erica as Malcolm's high-mileage Mini Minor rolled down the drive.

"You've made the conquest that counts," said Malcolm, a smile broadening his angular face as they left the grounds of Lady Gift and turned down a narrow lane with hedges on either side grown so high that it was like being in a shallow green canyon. "Kimberley has decided you're hers! It's rather sad for Peggie. Take care she doesn't poison your soup."

Alarm shot through Erica. She checked it quickly, annoyed with Malcolm for his lighthearted suggestion. "Peg is certainly attached to Kim, but she'll still see plenty of her. Besides, she says that Mr. Matthews has about decided to put Kim in boarding school if I leave. Doting on Kim as she does, it's to Peg's advantage for me to stay."

"Love takes peculiar shapes," Malcolm platitudinized amiably. "Rather than see you take her place in Kim's heart, Peg might prefer to lose the child to an abstract like a school—just as some lovers can accept the death of the beloved, even cause it, before they'll lose the person to someone else."

"I don't see much point into going into all this," Erica said, unable to keep sharpness from her tone.

Malcolm shrugged, his bronze layered hair settling impeccably into place. "Forewarned is forearmed. No one so deaf as she who will not hear."

Erica turned on him. "Will you please say what you're driving at?"

"Dear lady, I've tried!" They were coasting through the village. "There's the post office-general store," pointed out Malcolm. "The church dates from Saxon times and has a ghost, of course, a monk who seduced local maidens till an irate father scythed his head off his shoulders."

"There are so many ghosts in a country like this that there's hardly room for the living." Erica began the sentence in sarcasm and ended it pensively.

Malcolm cast her a quick look as they parked by a

thatched white-washed pub. "You say truer than you know!" he said, more gently than he had yet spoken. His hand gave hers a reassuring squeeze. "Never mind the ghosts, Erica. Keep your eye on the live ones!"

"If you know something—"

"Look, all I know is that three of the previous ladies engaged for Kim came to me utterly convinced that their lives were in danger. One even swore she was seeing a ghost—our handless Lady Margaret, you know—and that it had tried to push her down the stairs."

"Difficult for a handless ghost," joked Erica, but the muscles around her mouth were stiff.

"That's what Angier told her, but she left."

Malcolm came around to help Erica out of his tiny red car. They passed under the sign of a distrait Saint Peter tugging at a long beard, and into a low-ceilinged long room with a bar running its length. Men stood along it, drinking their shandy or bitter, while mugs of all sizes, pewter, copper, glass or pottery, hung from hooks in the ceiling beams, ready to the grasp of a perspiring, efficient tall girl whose towering blonde hairdo could only be a wig.

Seats ran along the opposite windows and chairs were grouped around scattered tables where some couples were having snacks or sipping their drinks and chatting. Malcolm ducked to lead Erica into a smaller room where meals were being served.

"Thank God, we'll have a meal without Caitlyn launching into a diatribe about the tribulations of whatever creature supplied our meat!"

Malcolm seated Erica so that she faced the room with its fireplace and horse brasses gleaming along the heavy brown ceiling beams. The tablecloth and napkins were snowy white and a single yellow rose blushed with pink emitted a sweet fragrance. "The roast duckling is usually very spot-on, the lamb with mint sauce excellent, the soup homemade and good, and the gooseberry crumble is the best I've ever eaten," Malcolm recommended.

Erica laughed. "I'll leave it to you," she said. "You seem to know what you're talking about!"

They had mulligatawny, duckling with orange sauce, new potatoes, broad beans, and gooseberry crumble with thick Devon cream. Malcolm was very much the gracious host, making small talk through dinner, getting Erica to talk about herself. When the coffee came, he settled back and made a bridge of his hands, on which he rested his long chin as he considered Erica.

"Your work permit is being sorted out by the proper authorities and I don't expect any snags. I understand you wish to send money to the States for your mother, and we can arrange a standing order at the bank for part of your salary to be transferred monthly to wherever you like."

Erica gave him the name and address of her mother's hospital and filled in the forms he produced from a slim folder taken from inside his coat.

"Now," he said, "driving! A man from the Maidendown School can give you several lessons a week, but I should think it easier for me to take you out for a daily run, say right after lunch."

"That's very kind of you, but I don't want to be a nuisance."

He flashed the singularly charming grin that made his bony face seem much younger, gave her hand a pat. "Erica, my dear! Going about with you will be a pleasure—and a blessed change from most of my work! Shall we start tomorrow?"

Erica gave a mock shudder. "The sooner the better, I suppose. I'm afraid it will take me a long time not to keep on the right!"

"You'll see the other traffic and that'll help you keep in the proper lane," soothed Malcolm. "Your main trouble will be at roundabouts and when you turn off one road onto another." He glanced at his watch and sighed. "Time to get back to the fortress. I've got to have some reports ready for Angier first thing in the morning. Sybil should have done them, but the darling girl has a way of leaving the sticky wickets to me."

"It seems strange for her to be Mr. Matthews' secretary."

"It was stranger when she was his wife!"

"But surely she—" Erica broke off. The relationships at Lady Gift were so tangled it was hard to know what to say to anyone.

"You mean she's a terribly efficient, broad-minded person to carry on?" Malcolm snorted. "She's only there to keep an eye on her interests—and of course Angier allows it because he can mark her wages off against tax instead of paying alimony. It's not a healthy situation! If I had my way, Angier would leave Sybil to hold down Lady Gift and himself live in London and New York where he'd be in touch with theater realities. But he buries himself down here in the muck of his past and then wonders why he can't write another hit!"

"I hope you don't consider Kim part of the muck!"

Malcolm's eyebrows climbed. "So you've taken to her? That's good. If Angier felt she had a competent mother-surrogate, he wouldn't be so obsessed with staying near her. Dear Erica, I have great respect and fondness for our Kimberley. But at this time being around her only torments Angier. It's a kind of penance—an offering to the dead! And I'm sure you'd agree that sort of guilt-enforced bond is not good for Angier or the child."

"I don't know enough about it to make judgments," said Erica slowly. "But you can be sure I'll do my best with Kim."

"Nobody could say fairer than that," nodded Malcolm, but Erica, preceding him to the car, wished he had either said nothing about the involvements at Lady Gift, or a good deal more.

His hand, as he helped her into the car, lingered just a trifle longer than necessary. Second-nature gallantry? In spite of his manner of pleasant frankness, Erica wondered how far he could be trusted, jumped as he spoke.

"Why the deep silence?"

She forced a laugh. "I must be catching Lady Gift fever—galloping assumptions!"

He chuckled, slanting her a quick glance of appreciation. "Just don't rush your hurdles. I think, Erica, that you'll improve Lady Gift tremendously!"

He walked her to the door, unlocked it, and brushed the lightest kiss on her forehead before going to garage the car.

As Erica climbed the stairs, she could hear Peg and Kim from the open-doored kitchen. "When the Catholic girl came off the rack," said Kim, in hushed tones of mingled horror and curiosity, "she was all pulled out of her sockets!"

"Her socks, you say? And was she six feet tall or six and a half?"

"Then they burnt her at the stake," persisted Kim.

"Rare or well done?" teased Peg.

Erica reflected in wry shock that Peg's ancestors had flocked happily to the gallows and public quarterings, that along with her stolid good nature she had inherited a sort of callousness, or simply a lack of imagination or ability to believe in the suffering of persons separated from her by time or space.

Yet an ordinary English soldier had made that little cross to comfort Joan of Arc.

"Bedtime," Erica announced to Kim, who was perched on a stool sipping milk. "Thanks for looking after her, Peg."

"I don't have to be thanked for staying with my poppet," Peg said with dignity. She pressed the child to her full bosom. "Good night, love! Sweet dreams." She went out with a last smile for Kim, but not a flicker of one for Erica.

Erica tucked Kim into bed, entered her room and started at the sight of Peg perched ludicrously on the edge of the chaise longue, rather like an albatross roosting on a nut shell.

"Miss Erica, you have to know this! That nasty St. Clair woman, I caught her giving Kimmy biscuits today—biscuits that were purely a baked paste of ground nuts!"

Erica frowned. "Well, Peg—"

"You don't understand?" Peg managed to sneer and look frightened at the same instant. "And you're supposed to be a mother to my poppet! Why, she's so allergic to nuts that a speck of one makes her cough and wheeze till she gets sick to her stomach and chucks it all up! A biteful of that biscuit would have sent

Kimmy to hospital choking almost to death!"

"But why should Miss St. Clair want to make Ki[m]
sick?"

"She could hope to bring on a reaction so bad
would kill my lamb! Or at least make Mr. Angier thi[nk]
Kim should live in a school-hospital for asthma[tic]
young ones."

"Peg, are you sure Miss St. Clair knows Kim[is]
allergic to nuts?"

"Sure she does! Because she's got all these cra[zy]
food notions, and she's always telling Mrs. Shell th[at]
Kim would get over her allergies if we fed her lots [of]
eggs and nuts and all the things that make her sick. S[he]
claims Kim would get used to the foods and be [all]
right—and of course, that's what she said when I fou[nd]
her sneaking the nut biscuit to Kim—that she was on[ly]
trying to help!"

"Well, I'd better speak to her," said Erica.

"Indeed you had!" Confident outer mann[er]
collapsing, Peg put her face in her hands and sobbe[d.]

"Why, Peggie, what's wrong?" Erica asked.

"I couldn't bear it if anything happened to Kimm[y,"]
Peg wept.

"Nothing will," soothed Erica, touched by su[ch]
devotion but hoping it could be moderated.

Peg flung her head back, eyes streaming. "Tha[t's]
easy to say! That's what they said about me twin sist[er]
too—only person ever loved me till I found the popp[et.]
But me sister died of a fever. And then my elder sis[ter]
was my mum's pet and my brother was my da[d's]
favorite, and I had no one! Not till Kim!"

Jumping up with amazing speed for her size, Peg [put]
her face close to Erica. "I could watch her better th[an]

nyone! Haven't I slept outside her door like a watchdog? But Mr. Angier, he's got these notions I'm too common to be in charge of Kim. Well, mind you look after her, my American lady! I'll know who to blame if things go wrong now that I've warned you!"

She swept out, leaving Erica to wonder how much of her concern was overheated imagination and jealousy, how much had real cause. Erica shrank from believing that anyone, however warped, would hurt Kim, but she had better have a talk with Caitlyn, and keep a vigilant watch till she knew more about the deep underground currents that flowed at Lady Gift.

Caitlyn was not at breakfast, an event celebrated by brighter conversation. Sybil, told of the state of Kim's wardrobe, offered to drive Erica and Kim into town about mid-morning.

They left after a mercifully short bout with the multiplication tables. Sybil, who was being cordial but not saying much, got her hair done while Erica and Kim shopped for everything from shoes to bathing suit to party clothes, though they bought mostly easy-care play mix-and-matchers. Erica also bought wire to secure the loft ladder and a sharp vine pruner at the big Woolworth's, while Kim selected toffees and humbugs.

After lunch, again a meal happier for Caitlyn's absence, Peg and Kim went swimming while Erica slid under the wheel of Malcolm's car and braved her first lesson.

Patient, unflappable and good-humored, Malcolm proved an ideal instructor, coaching Erica with exactitude and forethought so that she didn't have to make sudden decisions about lanes at this stage.

"Pull in at the Beard," he told her as they hummed back through the village after almost an hour. "You've earned a drink!"

They spent a bantering fifteen minutes in the pub. Malcolm kept the mood light and most of Erica's fleeting mistrust of the night before evaporated. Everyone else at Lady Gift seemed nervous. Why shouldn't he be?

Back at the house, with an hour to spare till Kim was her responsibility, Erica decided not to attack the ivy today, but to fasten the loft ladder and slip in a bit of work on her thesis.

She took the wire, went down the gallery to the loft closet and discovered the light was on. Had someone forgotten to switch it off, or were Kim and Peg on the sun roof?

Erica climbed the long ladder, knelt and secured it to uprights that reached to the ceiling. She tested the ladder, found it no longer tended to sway back, and nodded her satisfaction.

She would just see if anyone was on the roof. If it was deserted, she would turn off the light as she left the closet.

Along the catwalk she moved, toward the eave window. It was not hooked and hung slightly ajar. Stepping out, she found the roof unoccupied, looked behind the long chimney to be sure Kim hadn't curled up there, then turned to go back.

Someone had certainly been careless. If it rained with this window hanging open— Bright color caught her eye. Gripped by sudden fear, she caught her breath and moved toward the edge.

t took her a horrible moment to realize that the color
hat had alerted her was the flame of Caitlyn's bikini.
The actress lay unmoving on the paved court.

Erica screamed, started to scream again, fought
down her panic and dashed through the window, along
he catwalk to the ladder. All her movements seemed
naddeningly slow, clumsy.

Maybe Caitlyn was still alive. She must have slipped.
Or—hideous but inescapable thought—she could have
urled herself down!

Choked with dread, Erica reached the bottom of the
adder, wrenched open the closet and ran to Angier's
oor.

Angier had started up from his desk, scowling at
eing burst in upon, but before Erica panted out all the
ory, he was dialing.

"Doctor Dunwoodie? Angier Matthews. We've had
n accident—may be quite serious, can you come right
ow and send an ambulance? A fall—three stories
nto hard paving—haven't looked yet myself. Right,
e won't move her. Right! Thanks!"

He cradled the phone, snatched blankets off the bed,
nd caught Erica's wrist, sweeping her through the
allery, down the stairs, and out through a little
assage that opened on the inner court.

"Caitlyn!" he shouted, eyes blazing as he dropped to his knees. "Caitlyn, have you finally done it?"

The woman lay absolutely still, arms outflung as if she had tried to break her fall. Blood had dried at her mouth, was starting to crust in a small pool under her face. Angier put his ear close to her lips, touched the artery at the side of her throat, slowly got to his feet.

"So she really did it," he said in a strained, husky voice. "I never thought she would—"

"She may have slipped." The air seemed brilliant crystal, a too clear illusion that would shatter in a moment. Erica's tongue stuck to the roof of her mouth. She swallowed and went on, "Caitlyn's been sunbathing on the roof. She could have lost her footing."

"She jumped," said Angier flatly. A spasm of pain made his face twist. He turned from the body as if wracked with intolerable feeling. "There must have been something I could have done! Something I could have got her to do! I knew she was unbalanced. But I thought if I could finish the play and get her back in a big hit, the fame and adulation could lessen her hurt in—in realizing I would not marry her. Maybe I should have let her hope till the play was in rehearsal, but she clung—oh God, how she clung! I had to get loose!"

Enough to push this woman at their feet over the ledge? Angier stiffened, regaining control as if he read the involuntary question in Erica's mind. "Come into the library. We'll wait for the doctor there. And I suppose I'll have to call the police."

Doctor Dunwoodie, bluff, bearded, and grey-haired, was there by the time Angier had phoned the Maidendown constabulary.

"I would guess that she's been dead several hours,

Mr. Matthews," said the doctor, shaking his head regretfully as he rose from examining Caitlyn. "House guest, wasn't she?"

Angier nodded. "I don't know of any relatives or close friends."

"Pity," growled Dunwoodie. "Fine figure of a woman, and just in her prime! Actress, wasn't she? Think I've seen her in your plays."

"Quite likely."

"Anybody see her fall?" asked Dunwoodie.

"She jumped," Angier said positively.

Dunwoodie flinched, turned to stare up at the roof. "Jumped? Why?"

"She hated me." Angier's voice was heavy. "She was on the edge of insanity; this was the only way her sick mind saw to hurt me."

Dunwoodie's jaw dropped. "Easy, old chap! Better not come out with such talk! Doesn't sound right, you know, with the poor woman lying there all smashed up!"

The police arrived just ahead of the ambulance in the persons of a thin, tall, blond constable and a stocky, red-bearded, green-eyed detective sergeant in plain clothes. After a careful study of Caitlyn, chalk marks defining her position, and a trip up to the roof, they let the ambulance take the body. Dunwoodie made his report and left.

"Can we just sit down and ask a few questions, sir, of you and your household?" asked the sergeant.

Angier's lips tightened, but he waved the policemen into the library.

"Now, Miss Hastings, you found the body—saw it from the roof, as you've told us." The green eyes swung up abruptly. "What were you doing up there?"

Erica felt blood rise to her face, knew she couldn't have looked more guilty if she had been. "I—I had wired the ladder, which was unsteady, and wondered why the light was on. Before I turned it off, I wanted to be sure no one was sunbathing, so I looked out on the roof."

"And just happened to glance down in the court?"

"I had crossed over to see if anyone was behind the chimney and was leaving the roof when the red of—of Miss St. Clair's suit caught my eye."

"Who used the roof for sunbathing?

"So far as I know, Mr. Matthews' daughter Kim, and Peg, who works here, were the only ones besides Miss St. Clair."

The officer glanced at Angier. "Does this agree with your knowledge, sir?"

"I don't know who uses the roof," said Angier. He thrust his hair back wearily. "What I feel fairly sure of is that Miss St. Clair jumped."

The constable's eyebrows shot up. "What makes you think that, Mr. Matthews?"

"She was not a happy person."

"Really, sir, neither are thousands of people, but they don't jump off roofs."

Angier shrugged.

"If you know of any specific thing that might have provoked Miss St. Clair into a suicidal state, sir, surely you will tell us," persisted the green-eyed detective.

"She was depressed about her career and her—her private life," Angier muttered.

"Had she made any threats? Said anything to indicate that she was desperate?"

"Caitlyn was a desperate-sounding woman anytime she didn't like a situation!"

"How desperate, sir?" put in the thin young constable.

Angier's lips thinned. "She tried to drown herself only day before yesterday."

"There were witnesses?"

"Miss Hastings, my daughter, several gardeners, and I," said Angier, with an encompassing wave of his arm.

The red-bearded detective switched his gaze to Erica.

"Tell me how it was, please, Miss."

"Kim and I found Miss St. Clair floating face down in the pool. I got her out and Mr. Matthews revived her. But—"

"But what, Miss Hastings?"

Erica had a miserable sense of betraying Angier, but she owed it to the dead Caitlyn to tell what she could. "Miss St. Clair insisted that she had been napping in ordinary clothes—that someone had dressed her in the bikini and put her in the water."

The detective glanced frostily at Angier. "Did you know about this, sir?"

"Oh, Caitlyn swore she hadn't attempted suicide," Angier admitted. He didn't look at Erica. She was sure he was angry with her for raising an awkward matter. "But I could scarcely credit that!"

"Why not, Mr. Matthews?" probed the detective.

"Because she had faked attempts on her life before," Angier said reluctantly.

"When and how?"

"Twice in the past three months. The first time she pretended she had been gassed. The next time," he concluded tiredly, "she said she was poisoned. I rushed her to hospital in the middle of the night to have her stomach pumped."

"What makes you so sure she arranged these events?"

"Because she told me so herself. Both times she had hoped to shock me into doing what she wished. My secretary and accountant heard her confess the trickery."

"You didn't report these—attempts?"

"I thought the gassing was a simple accident. Caitlyn was always leaving taps running, cigarettes burning, fires on when they should be off, and so on. But after the poison uproar, I started to call the police, and that was when she begged me not to—said that she had taken a lot of sleeping pills in order to frighten me. Probably I was wrong, but she pleaded and promised till I thought it best to let the whole crazy business fade away."

The officer stroked his flaming beard a long moment, watching Angier who stared back with at least surface calm. "Well, sir," mused the officer, "whether her death was murder, accident or suicide, Miss St. Clair seems to have been most unhappy. Can you say why she wanted to—shock you? What did she want you to do?"

"She wanted me to marry her," Angier said bluntly. "As you may know, Miss St. Clair had starred in some of my plays. We had an association, which I felt had to end when it became clear that she wanted marriage. I trust you gentlemen will agree that a person's marital choices are eminently his own business!"

"Yet she was often a guest at Lady Gift," murmured the policeman.

A haunted look of regret and guilt flashed in Angier's eyes. "She—had nowhere else to go; no one else to stay with. Or rather, she was reckless with money when she had it so that when she wasn't working, she was always quickly destitute."

"A woman like that could become a burden and a menace," suggested the officer.

"She was." Angier hunched his shoulders, but the look he gave the policeman was direct and straightforward. "She reckoned that I had failed her both as a playwright and potential husband. Instead of finding better examples of both, she seemed able only to stay down here and keep us both on edge and miserable!" Angier stuck his hands in his pockets and faced the fireplace. "Looking back, I don't see where I could have done differently with the knowledge I had at each step of involvement. But it's a terrible thing to feel partly to blame for another person's death, even if she was on the thin edge of madness. I'm as sure as I can be that her suicide was vengeance on me."

"There's some doubt that it was suicide, sir. We will post a guard on the roof till one of our experts has been out to check. You and Miss Hastings may go now, but I shall need to talk to everyone who's been in the house today."

Angier frowned, then shrugged. "I'll tell my secretary to get everybody. Do you need the gardeners and dailies?"

"Everybody, sir. We won't cause more disturbance than necessary."

A sudden thought sent dismay across Angier's face. "Surely you won't need to see my daughter. She's only nine!"

"Sorry, Mr. Matthews, I'm afraid we'll have to have a word with her. Don't worry, we generally get on better with children than with their folks!" The red-beard drooped one eyelid and chuckled.

Angier buzzed Sybil on the intercom, told her what was wanted, and turned to Erica. "Can you find Kim? I'd like her to answer her questions first and get out of this!"

Kim was not upstairs, nor in the pool, but Erica found her in the butler's pantry, sipping weak tea and crunching biscuits, as Peg joked with the gardeners who were enjoying their afternoon break.

"I think you'll all be wanted around in the front hall soon," Erica warned as the men sprang up. "Come along, Kim."

"See you later, poppet!" called Peg to the child, favoring Erica with a cool, almost impudent smile as she poured more tea for the men. "Wonder what Mr. Angier wants to tell us, lads? Maybe the gov'ment has levied some more bloody taxes!"

If she had any hint of what the household was being summoned for, she didn't show it. She would scarcely grieve for Caitlyn, anyway. Kim bolted her tea and went with Erica, still eating the crumbly rich shortbreads.

"It's too late for lessons, isn't it, Eric?" she pleaded, hanging back as they approached the library.

"You just need to answer a few questions, dear." Erica gave the child a reassuring hug and brought her into the library. Kim's eyes widened as she saw the constable's uniform.

"Hello, young lady," greeted the officer. "Take a seat!" He smiled at Erica. "You may stay, too, madam."

He questioned Kim kindly and swiftly. Did she go to the roof often? Had she been there that day? Not at all?

102

Then when? With whom? With Miss Hastings on the day before yesterday? Had she ever slipped or lost her footing on the roof? Oh, she had slipped on a tile once? But Peg had saved her. . . .

She spent a lot of time with Peg? They had been together ever since lunch because Miss Hastings had gone on a driving lesson? And they had gone swimming and then had tea?

Had they seen anyone since lunch? Only the gardeners. Not Miss St. Clair? No, in fact no one had seen Miss St. Clair all day, she hadn't come to any meals.

"Thank you very much," the policeman told Kim, bowing as he escorted her and Erica to the door.

Peg, the gardeners, Malcolm, Mrs. Shell and the two daily women were seated about the hall under Sybil's managerial eye. Erica nodded to them, piloted Kim through their curious looks, and went up the stairs.

"What is it?" Kim demanded. "Why did the policeman come? Why did that man with the red beard ask all those questions?"

Erica took a long breath. The child would have to know. "Caitlyn slipped off the roof. She's dead."

"Dead?" Kim froze at the top of the stairs, face going chalk white. "You mean she fell off—just—just the way I hoped she would?" The last words rose in terror.

Erica gripped thin shoulders, gave Kim a shake. "We all say things we don't mean! Come along, I'll make you a nice Horlick's—"

"I—I said I hoped she'd fall!"

"Yes, I know, but that didn't cause the accident, Kim! It had nothing to do with it!"

Kim's frantic eyes searched Erica's. "Are you sure?"

"Of course!" Erica hadn't wanted to bring in the chance of suicide, but under the circumstances it seemed the best idea. "Caitlyn may have jumped, Kim. She's supposed to have tried to hurt herself other times. Anyway, what you said had nothing to do with it!"

Kim let herself be steered to the kitchen. She trembled, seemingly dazed, as Erica heated milk and added the powder, then coaxed her to sip it.

"I wish—I wish I hadn't said that! About her falling—" Kim muttered.

"It was natural enough," Erica reasoned. "Now, Kim, you must stop worrying about that! It had nothing to do with Caitlyn's dying."

The dark grey eyes fastened on Erica. "Then you don't believe what Peg says?"

"What does Peg say?"

Kim licked her lips. "She says you can wish somebody dead."

"That's nonsense!"

"She says she's known it to happen," Kim insisted with stubborn misery.

Damn Peg with her ghosts and superstitions! As if there wasn't enough real trouble around this place! Erica cradled Kim's head against her and spoke as earnestly and emphatically as she could.

"Kim, people have died of fright. I do think if an easily upset person found out that someone was wishing them dead or sticking pins in a doll meant to represent them, or casting spells to harm them, then that person might get so nervous and worried they would die—but only because their fear took over. Now you weren't casting spells or threatening Caitlyn or—"

"Yes, I was!" cried the child.

Erica's heart stopped. "What do you mean, Kim?"

"I was afraid she'd get Angier to send me to boarding school," the girl wept. "I—I'd sort of imagine I was talking to Lady Margaret, and I'd ask her to make Caitlyn leave! Maybe—" Kim's eyes dilated and her voice broke as she gripped Erica's hands. "Maybe Lady Margaret pushed her off!"

"Kim!" Erica held the child till the paroxysm of guilt and fear had eased. "There is no Lady Margaret! You had nothing to do with whatever happened to Caitlyn. Now come into my room and read till dinnertime."

"Can—can I sleep with you tonight?"

"If you want to, I'll put you on the chaise," Erica promised. "Now don't worry, Kim. You had no fault in this, and I'll help you all I can. You won't be alone or afraid."

Erica shooed Kim down the gallery, assuming all the brisk normality she could, but she herself was troubled and afraid.

She certainly didn't believe in ghosts, but there was an aura of pain and remembered grief at Lady Gift that was beginning to weigh upon her like a gigantic, slowly increasing pressure. If there were no ghost murderer, then there was at least the possibility of a human one. And in any case, it was awful to know that a woman, beautiful and talented, was dead and there had been no one to call but the police and the doctor—no one to care.

Angier, for the first time during Erica's stay, was at dinner that night. He seated Kim, who clapped her hands together in pleasure at his presence, and proceeded to carve the joint onto the heated plates which Peg rushed around to the diners.

The place where Caitlyn had sat was absorbed by placing Malcolm and Erica further apart. As Angier took his seat, Malcolm raised his wine glass.

"Here's to poor Cait! May she be happier wherever she is than ever she was on earth! She should enjoy the splash all the London papers are giving her demise!"

No one else drank to his toast. Looking a touch embarrassed he bolted the wine and coughed. "At least now we can enjoy our meat!"

"We might if you could talk about something pleasant," Sybil cut in. But she immediately turned on Angier and said with violence, "I always told you it was a mistake to let Caitlyn stay here, that being near you only fed her impossible fantasies! She even told around the village that you were secretly married! If you couldn't get her to leave, you might at least have made her see a psychiatrist!"

"Steady, old girl," soothed Malcolm.

Sybil glared at him, swung to Angier, and again accused him with her pale blue eyes. "I hope you'll learn from this, Angier! The kind of theatrical people you're constantly meeting are not good living companions. It's not fair to me to bring them here and make me cope with them—"

"Drop it, Sybil!" Angier commanded. "Any time you'd rather find another job, go ahead. Now let's have no more discussion of Caitlyn! We've called in the police and doctor, they'll complete the investigation, and that will only prove what I'm sure of."

"Ah, yes," murmured Malcolm. "The doctor and police! That's our modern way of laying the ghost— the stake of reason we drive through the hearts of corpses that might otherwise rise up and walk—"

"Oh, stop it!" cried Erica, putting her hand on Kim's shoulder. The child looked positively haunted. "Don't any of you ever remember that you're speaking before a child?"

"Sorry." Malcolm flashed Kim a melting smile. "Is that one of your new outfits, Kimberley? Most attractive!"

She was wearing a brightly patterned jersey jump-suit with bell bottoms, which she had gloated over in the shop and put on as soon as they got home, but even a compliment from a grown-up could not cheer her. She nodded to the question and stared sickly at her food.

Suddenly, hands burying her face, Sybil burst into weeping. "It's horrible! I always knew—knew something dreadful would happen!"

Angier slammed down his knife. "Sybil, this happens—you always find an excuse to cry—when I try to dine at my own table! You be pleasant at meals or have a tray in your room, do you understand?"

"Y—yes, Angier." Sybil's shoulders heaved a few times, but when she put down her napkin, her smile was bright, and except for redness about the eyes, one would have thought her happy.

What was the matter with all of them? The three had been together fifteen years. Their intimacy was to Erica a dark boundary beyond which she could not see, behind which events transpired in another, hidden dimension, just as there was at Lady Gift a dimension of pain and old grief that was almost palpable.

Maybe there was no room in such a house for life or joy or love. . . .

Feeling as if cold fingers had shut around her heart, Erica glanced at Kim, who was watching her with grey eyes at once troubled and hopeful.

Nothing must hurt Kim. Somehow, for her, Lady Gift must become a house of the living, not of the dead—or the bright soullessness of Sybil's chatter brought on by Angier's angry rebuke. Erica didn't wait for coffee but excused herself along with Kim.

"Could we go out to the Barracks?" Kim asked. "I don't feel like staying inside these long days when it stays light so long. Are your summer days this long in Houston, Eric?"

"No, Kimmie. And our winter days aren't as short as yours must be."

"I don't mind winter," Kim said amazingly. "It's going to bed when it's still daylight that I hate! When I grow up, I think I'll live in America."

"When you grow up, you can go to bed whenever you want to," Erica laughed. "And you'll want to!"

They walked under the deep green canopy of the Douglas fir, relishing the tangy smell of the needles which were springy under their feet, picking up especially nice cones. Then Kim wandered down to the graceful little wych elm while Erica lingered at the overgrown rockery with its sundial.

She had never seen one up close before and climbed precariously over shifting rocks to look down at the tarnished brass face with its spidery numerals and marker.

She tried to move the marker, realized that it was fixed, not only by construction but the corrosion and rust of weather and years.

"You can't change it," said a voice behind her. Erica whirled like a guilty child to face Angier who stood with his hands in his pockets, smiling. "Does it go against your American optimism to tell time by shadows?"

"There can't be shadows without sun," she retorted. "We call it a sundial, not a shadow dial!"

"Bravely spoken!" He cleared the distance between them. The rocks didn't slip beneath his feet, but she heard one grind into powder. He stood gazing down at her, his eyes questioning—pleading?—though his tone was flippant. "Then may I hope that a woman who marks time by sun instead of shadow, in spite of all the evidence, will hold the fort? Stand by her guns, not show the white feather?"

She frowned. He caught her wrist. His palm pressed the veins and she hoped he could not detect the leaping of her pulse.

"I mean, Miss Hastings, that I trust the—the accident, the lurid publicity, and our perhaps disagreeable company won't put you off. You seem right for Kim." Almost humbly he released Erica. "I couldn't blame you if you decided to run. But I hope you'll stay—and make Lady Gift a home for Kim."

And you? Erica wondered suddenly. She had been angered at his apparent lack of sympathy for Caitlyn, but he seemed tired; weary unto death, wasn't that the phrase? Who could know what went on between a man and a woman, withering affection, killing respect? Angier was master of Lady Gift, but he seemed more trapped there than anyone, imprisoned by his past, surrounded by it, as Pluto, Lord of the Dead, was condemned to live among shades.

And Pluto, lonely, had found a girl to brighten his dead kingdom; ravished away from her mother, she had pined till the dark ruler let her return to the living.

But the seed she had eaten meant that she must spend half of every year among the dead. . . .

Skin prickling, Erica turned from the sundial and the tall black-haired man to look for Kim, who, sighting her father, ducked out from under the wych elm and ran towards them.

Angier, without waiting for Erica's answer, turned abruptly and walked away.

IX

Kim faltered, stopped as if she had been forcibly checked. Furious at Angier, puzzled at his veering moods, Erica put her arm around Kim.

"Goodness, it's bedtime! Shall we make the chaise into a couch for Sleeping Beauty?"

"You mean I can be the princess?" cried Kim, allowing herself to be diverted.

"Yes. In fact, your lessons tomorrow can be making up a play, writing it down, and putting it on."

"Who'll be the audience?"

"I will. And Peg would enjoy it."

"Lovely!" Kim glowed, but she sounded a bit wistful and Erica's determination hardened. Angier must come, too. He had to do more for his daughter than loom peripherally at the edges of her life, shadowing but never lighting it.

Soon Kim, cuddling her doll Lady Margaret, lay nestled among pillows and coverlets on the chaise with the silver swan bending its graceful neck toward her. She smiled and held up her arms to Erica in a gesture of such love and trust that Erica had to blink back tears as she kissed the child good-night and wished her sweet dreams.

But her own sleep was haunted with images of Caitlyn, broken against the paving. Had she fallen?

Had she thrown herself over, literally and deliberately dying at Angier's door? Or was it faintly possible that someone had pushed her?

The red-bearded detective was back next day with several specialists, but they did whatever they needed to do and went their way without asking any more questions.

Erica helped Kim design clothes for her play and stitched miniature sables and velvets for Anne Boleyn and Henry the Eighth, while Kim nibbled at her pen and scrawled dialogue.

"I'll end with Anne learning that a French headsman has been imported for her," Kim decided, flexing ink-stained fingers. "She will touch her throat, laugh, and say, 'It's such a little neck!' and then she'll walk out of her cell, very proudly, like this. . . ." Holding the doll, Kim glided forward in barefooted, scratch-legged majesty, turned to Erica eagerly. "Do you think that's a good ending?"

"Yes, if it matches what goes before."

"Eric, do you think Henry loved Anne?"

"In his way, he must have."

"Then how could he kill her? A man couldn't kill a woman he loved in these days, could he?"

"I suppose it happens. Now see if you can finish your script before lunch."

Kim did, and brought up flowers from the herbaceous border. She loved to gather them and almost daily gifted Erica, Peg and Mrs. Shell with bouquets; but never Sybil, nor Caitlyn when she had been alive.

Malcolm, instead of letting Erica concentrate on driving, seemed driven to ask her one question after another about Caitlyn and how she had been discovered.

"You didn't hear anything that made you go out on the roof?" he asked. "Or see anything—a shadow —some movement?"

"I've told you half a dozen times!" Erica snapped. "The light had been left on and I didn't want to leave anyone stumbling around in the dark!"

"You certainly are touchy!"

"Well, why do you keep on? I've told you all I can!"

"Sometimes a person forgets some tiny but important detail."

"Let's please leave the investigation to the police," Erica suggested curtly. "Which arrow do I follow at the roundabout?"

"The middle one. It forks us into town." Malcolm settled into directing her, though his manner was abstracted. Erica was too intent on keeping to the left and dodging buses, lorries and multitudinous bicycles, to think much about him till they were back at his garage. As she switched off the engine and gave him the key, he closed his hand over hers for a minute.

"Erica, don't go out on that roof."

"But Kim likes to sunbathe there!"

"She'd better not go, either."

His hazel eyes drilled into Erica as if commanding obedience.

"Do—do you think Caitlyn was pushed?" Erica faltered.

"I'd swear she was."

"Why?"

He regarded her for a long, searching moment. "For all I know, you shoved her and are giving me the wide-eyed innocent bit!"

113

"Why would I do that? I scarcely knew her!"

"She was jealous of you. Afraid you might take Angier's fancy. It's possible that you and Cait met on the roof, she attacked and you fought her off. You might not have dreamed she would slip and fall—"

"If it happened, I'd have said so." Erica kept her voice under control but waves of cold alarm shot through her.

The hazel eyes glittered as if to force the truth from her, then softened as Malcolm turned his falcon's head and brooded. "I don't think you were up there with her," he conceded. "But I believe someone was—and that someone might kill you if they thought you might have seen them up there with Cait."

"If you suspect such a thing, why don't you tell the police?"

"Because I don't know who did it." Malcolm whirled on her. "Shocked? Yes, you'd think someone who kills must pay! But I lack your straightforward crime equals punishment convictions!"

"What do you mean?"

"I mean if Sybil or Peg or one of the gardeners pushed Cait, I'd jog our red-bearded investigator. But if it was Angier—" Malcolm hesitated, finished in a quieter tone. "If it was Angier, I wouldn't blame him!"

"What could possibly justify murder?"

"You have heard of self-defense?"

"But Caitlyn couldn't wrestle Angier off the roof!"

"Don't be so literal! She's been blackmailing Angier emotionally—and for all I know, financially—for years. She had clamped her tentacles on him till he couldn't move without her swaying along on top of him, looking ever so lovely and graceful but marking him with ugly weals where she held on. He should have

114

cut her loose long ago, but he felt obligated—"

"Why?"

"Because the plays she starred in made his reputation, and the crazy relationship between them inspired those plays to start with, that distilled pleasure-pain that gets taken for love so often these days because it's the only mixture that some people can feel." Malcolm shrugged. "Angier has an over-developed conscience. Look at the way he's kept Sybil on. Look at the way he insists on staying at Lady Gift because of Kim, when he'd be worlds better off professionally in London or New York."

"And how about you?" Erica asked abruptly. "Why are you so worried about Angier? Why do you care where he lives so long as you get your salary?"

Malcolm inclined his head to acknowledge the thrust, a tough little smile quirking his long mouth. "Angier is the friend of my youth. And my salary is more of a percentage. Which hasn't been too high of late."

"Maybe *you* pushed Caitlyn."

The impeccably layered hair shifted as Malcolm laughed and shook his head. "I was with someone all the time yesterday, and can prove it. That's more, I'll wager, than you can do!"

"I don't have to prove it," Erica retorted.

"Not yet," he said blandly, raised a hand as she started to protest. "I believe you! Enough to repeat, my dear: don't go out on that roof!"

He thrust the key in his pocket and went whistling up the walk.

The papers soon found a new sensation and dropped Caitlyn's death. Life gradually came back to normal.

Kim took it for granted that she was to go on sleeping in Erica's room, and though Kim was scarcely a restful roommate, being given to tossing about and muttering, Erica could not send her out.

"Why do you get in your own bed long enough to tousle it up?" she asked Kim one morning, as they folded up the bedding from the chaise longue and stowed it in a closet.

"I don't want anyone to know I'm not sleeping there," Kim said, flushing. "Especially not Peg! She'd call me a baby!"

So they kept their sleeping arrangements a secret. Kim's pretense bothered Erica a little, but she told herself it was harmless compared to some riddles in this house. Besides, Peg would be even more jealous if she knew Kim slept by Erica, and though Erica couldn't believe the big cheery girl would do murder, one inhabitant of Lady Gift had died in strange circumstances, and there was Malcolm's warning—

Damn Malcolm! Erica usually thought at this stage of what seemed perpetual anxiety over Caitlyn's death and what might follow. He seemed as sure Caitlyn had been shoved as Angier was that she had leaped.

Or was Angier pretending?

Kim fed her fish twice daily, and liked to demonstrate proudly that the black mollies would nibble at her hand. "It's rather like the way a puppy would lick my hand, isn't it?" she asked several times. And once Erica caught her hugging the tank.

"I can't hold the fish any other way," Kim explained shamefacedly.

She was punctilious about changing the fiberglass filter weekly, siphoning sediment off the bottom of the tank now and then, and aging water overnight in a plastic bag to replace the amount that evaporated, so that the new water was the exact temperature of that in the tank. One morning she uttered a scream. Erica sped in to find her sobbing over a zebra fish who had got stranded on top of the plastic bag and died there.

The tiny corpse had been dried stiff by heat from the two bulbs that illuminated the small world of the aquarium. Sybil had been passing by and, oblivious of Erica, was murmuring softly to Kim, with one arm around her.

"That's what could happen to you, darling, if you don't take care with your breathing. You know when you have an attack, you can't breathe, anymore than the fish could. So you have to be very careful—"

She saw Erica then, and stepped quickly back from the child who buried her face against Erica.

"It's a pity about the fish." Sybil seemed thinner and looked extremely handsome in an aqua raw silk pants suit. "I was trying to get some good out of the little tragedy by reminding Kim to breathe properly."

"Under the circumstances, it seems more likely to frighten than help," Erica said over Kim's trembling shoulders.

Sybil gave her a long, strange look. "Sorry!" She clicked down the gallery and Erica rocked soothingly with the child.

"Never mind, dear. We'll go down to the aquarium and get a substitute—"

The word stung her lips. Substitute!

That was all Kim had! The fish, pretty and interesting but untouchable and isolated by glass and a foreign element, were substitutes for a pony or dog or kitten.

Instead of a mother, there was Peg. And a

succession of short-term companion-tutors! Angier had so little to do with the child that he was scarcely better than a make-shift—in a way, he was worse, because he was a real father who didn't act like one!

And the women he'd put around his daughter! Caitlyn, who had itched to send her off to boarding school and tried to feed her injurious foods; Sybil with her fear-engendering admonitions about breathing. Peg at least loved the child, but what could come from such a relationship as Kim grew older, if it was the only vital, living one she had? Should Peg, with her carefree tumbling and coarseness, be a model for Kim?

All this shot through Erica's mind in a few seconds, a crystallization of her several weeks at Lady Gift. Substitutes were better than nothing, weren't they?

Perhaps. If they didn't keep a person from preferring the real when it appeared. As Erica held Kim, she knew that must be her aim for the child—to replace substitutes with reality as much as possible.

Most particularly, to replace Angier's guilty, resentful concern for his child, a bond between father and daughter had to be nurtured, encouraged to grow as deep as it could, in honesty. And such a feeling could go deep, Erica was sure, once Angier dissolved the barriers that old griefs had built between him and the beautiful, lively child with her wealth of originality and verve. How could any father not adore her?

Erica checked the anger that was always ready to flare when she thought of Angier's coolness to his daughter. Putting him on the defensive wouldn't help, nor would arguments or reproaches. But by appealing to the mood he had shown that evening by the sundial, it should be possible to get him oftener into Kim's company, and once he saw more of her, he would have to respect her as a separate individual from his vanished wife.

Surely the painful memories would fade and he would come to love his daughter, find joy in her company, not sadness.

"Wash your face!" Erica told Kim. "Let's go see what we can find at the aquarium! And we'll stop at a book store and get a manual on yoga! Then you can show Sybil how to breathe!"

They brought home a yoga book and a pair of iridescent neon tetras, and that afternoon the mother black mollie spawned dozens of infinitesimal fry that resembled minute whales. Since the other fish, including the mother, were gobbling these as fast as they could, Erica caught the survivors and put them in a small subsidiary tank attached inside the big one.

"There must be fifty!" Kim gloated, crumbling fish food to a powder for her tiny new creatures. "I feel just like a mama!"

"I think when you grow up you'll decide there's a slight difference," Erica laughed. She left Kim playing soft tunes on her recorder to her freshly exciting aquarium, summoned her courage, and knocked at Angier's door.

There was no answer. What a nuisance! Just when she'd worked herself up to asking him to come to Kim's play! Disappointed, Erica was turning, when the door opened.

It was Sybil, still in the flattering silk tunic and pants. *Why not?* Erica demanded of herself. *She's his secretary!* Once, too, his wife. It would be more surprising than not, wouldn't it, if, living in the same house, they didn't sometimes revert to old habit?

"I'm sorry," Erica apologized. "I wanted to see Mr. Matthews about Kim."

"He's out at the moment." Sybil seemed friendly and regretful. "Shall I leave a note for him?"

"No, thanks. It's—involved, and I'll surely see him sometime soon."

Erica was a few steps down the gallery when Sybil called.

"Erica! Please come in a moment!"

An irrational urge to move on as if she hadn't heard flooded through Erica, but she checked it sternly and went back to Angier's room. Sybil closed the door.

And locked it.

Startled, Erica gripped the doorknob. Sybil noticed the gestures and her grim look vanished momentarily in a laugh. "Relax, my dear! Sit here and have a sherry! We've nothing to fear—at least not from each other."

Erica sat in a leather-cased chair, sipping the sherry Sybil produced from a small wall cabinet. Sybil belted down a jigger of straight whisky and followed it with another before she confronted Erica, her face seeming uncannily like one of the many masks in Angier's room.

"Erica," she said, with an appealing gesture, "I know you were off-put by what I said to Kim about breathing, but it is true, you know. If she learned to breathe properly, she could to a large extent control her asthma."

"I'm going to find out about beneficial exercises," Erica said.

"But you think my remarks did more harm than good?" Sybil raised a slim eyebrow, smiled and shrugged. "Possibly. In future, I'll leave Kim to you.

But my motives were helpful, I assure you."

Erica shifted restlessly, declined more sherry. Surely Sybil hadn't called her back in that frightened way and locked the door just to indulge in self-justification?

Moments passed, uneasy silence while Sybil fiddled with a golden charm bracelet. Erica felt oppressed by the masks staring at her from every angle, jeering, haunting, grotesque or menacing. Most of all she was troubled by the beautiful warm-skinned mask that Angier must gaze at each time he looked up from his desk. Erica put down her glass, started to rise.

"Wait!" Sybil pleaded, eyes swinging up. She moistened her lips. Words came in a rush. "Erica, that day you found Caitlyn—did you see anybody up there—hear anything?"

Not another inquisition!

"No. I just found her." It took effort but Erica kept her voice level. "That's all."

"Don't be angry!" Sybil bit her lip, hesitated, then spoke as if driven. "Angier stood to gain by Caitlyn's death. He had assigned a third of his royalties to her back when he was in love with her to compensate for the security of marriage he couldn't offer because of his duty to his child. Even when he pursued Caitlyn all over the Continent, he knew she wouldn't mother Kim, or even share him with her."

"But don't you have a similar arrangement with him?" Erica demanded.

Sybil grimaced. "Well, after all, I had been his wife. God knows I've kept his business affairs straight for fifteen years! That's worth something!" Her eyes met Erica's frankly. "When Angier fell in love with Kim's mother, he asked for a divorce and offered—I didn't ask!—very generous terms. So the situation was altogether different from the extortionate way in which Caitlyn exploited him."

"I don't quite see," said Erica, puzzled, "where all this is leading. None of it is any of my business, Sybil. Really, I'd rather not hear this kind of thing."

Sybil vented an abrupt laugh. "So you don't like suspicions cast on Angier!" she said, rising. She was definitely thinner and her breasts strained voluptuously at the raw silk as she paced to the window.

"Angier's not doing so well. He could use all the royalties himself, very handily. I know he had come to bitterly resent Caitlyn's taking her share—and I wouldn't be astonished if he grudges me mine!"

Erica rose. "This really is a private matter between you two!"

"It's a matter of justice," blazed Sybil. "I worked twelve hours a day at all the petty slave jobs so Angier could get where he is. I had precious little of the glamor or fun Kim's mother got to enjoy! He owes me at least a living—a damned good one! I won't release the copyrights. I'd die first!"

Her eyes widened. She began to laugh hysterically. "That was good! Maybe I will!" She came so close that Erica could smell the whisky. "Well, my little friend, I hoped maybe you had seen him on the roof or could offer some kind of evidence to set the police thinking." She gave a contemptuous laugh. "It seems you can't!"

Erica started for the door, fighting a chill constriction around her heart. "You need to go on a holiday," she told Sybil, bent to unlock the door.

Fingers, tipped with nails, dug into her shoulders. "So that's what you'd like?" Sybil gasped, her mouth distorted. "You think if you had him to yourself—"

Erica pulled free sharply enough to send the other woman reeling backwards.

Catching at the wall, Sybil stared accusingly. Harsh laughter tore from her throat. "Little Miss See-Nothing-Say-Nothing! Of course you wouldn't tell anything that might give him away, you want him yourself!"

"You're raving!"

Sybil came forward, almost crouching, her face now uglier than any of the masks. "You just remember that as I'm afraid now, you will be someday! Just as Caitlyn was! Just as—" Her eyes flicked involuntarily to the calm, lovely mask near the desk. The vitalizing anger left and her shoulders slumped. "Lady Gift won't be any safer for you than it has been for any woman. If you're clever, you'll go back to America!"

"I didn't see anything on the roof," Erica said, her hand on the doorknob. "Certainly I wouldn't let harm come to you—or anyone—if I could prevent it. But please remember that Caitlyn's fall was probably accidental or suicide."

"Do you really think so?" taunted Sybil, features heightened almost to beauty. "Run along, Erica, and study it as if your life depended on it—for someday it will!"

"I'd like to help you," Erica said. "But these absurd ideas—"

Sybil burst into laughter again, reaching for the whisky. Erica watched her helplessly for a moment, decided the older woman would quiet down better without an audience, and left.

X

Study it, Sybil had warned. Erica needed time to absorb and think about the whole thing, but put it from her while she selected some yoga exercises designed to aid breathing, and worked on them with Kim. They both liked the "Salutation to the Sun," which employed every part of the body in a graceful kind of ballet.

Later Erica left Kim at the pool with Peg, got her gloves and pruning tools and went to the Old Orchard.

The tree she had cleared of its strangling vines looked strange compared to the rest, and the nettles had grown waist-high in spots so that before she could start tearing ivy loose she had to flail a space around the next tree. She worked steadily for an hour, finished one tree, and began another, paused to rest a minute, leaning against the misshapen trunk and looking around this neglected place that seemed shut away, deliberately allowed to go to ruin.

Once the nettles must have been kept down. The scores of trees, planted in matched rows, would have been glorious in full blossom, or richly promising when laden with apples. Children could have climbed the trees and had their fruit fresh-plucked. A lover might have picked the nicest red apple for his sweetheart, held it temptingly high till ransomed with a kiss.

Erica sighed and came back to the present. Ridiculous to work at clearing it in the few hours she could snatch! Yet she felt that she could almost hear the trees begging for life, for air, sun, rain, freedom from the choking stranglers that curled to the highest branches, crept along each limb. She selected the biggest vine, pried under it with her bill hook, and yanked away.

"What are you doing here?"

Spinning, too surprised to answer, she stared at Angier who had come up without a sound. His grey eyes seemed to take in her, the tree, and what she was doing in a quick appraisal, but his tone was rougher than ever.

"Did you think yourself hired as a gardener, Miss Hastings? Where is Kim?"

"She's swimming with Peg." Erica flushed, wishing she didn't sound so guilty. "I hate to see the orchard like this. I didn't think it mattered if—"

"If you chopped your arm off or got properly stung by nettles?" His eyes twinkled suddenly, and it was startling how her heart lifted.

"I need some really active exercise," she defended. And stepped backwards into leaves that sent a fiery tingle up her arm. "Ohhh!" She held her stung wrist to her mouth, but Angier had broken off a large cucumberish-looking leaf and crushed it on the spot where clear blisters were rising.

"If you must wave your hands amid the nettles, you'd better learn what a dock leaf looks like! It'll take away the worst smarting."

But what could take away the warm thrill that went through her at his touch?

"Better?" he asked.

It took strong physical effort to withdraw her hand. "Much better," she said, with as much dignity as she could marshal. "Thank you."

One corner of his mouth turned down. "My pleasure, I assure you!" He looked around at the orchard.

The teasing lightness drained from his expression, leaving it bleak. He seemed to have forgotten Erica. His mouth set as his jaw hardened.

What made him look like that? What was there about this orchard to make it disgraced, shamed, left to die outside the walls and beyond the care of the gardeners?

"These trees are older than I am," he said. "They're hardly worth reclaiming. I suppose I should have them taken down."

"Oh, no!" cried Erica before she could stop herself. He swung to face her, jarred into remembering her presence.

"Why should you care?"

"I—I hate to see trees die."

"Even twisted, blighted, decaying old hulks?"

"They won't die if the vines come off! And Kim says the blossoms are lovely in May!"

He selected a small green apple that looked almost like a swollen knob. "But these are fruit trees, after all, Miss Hastings. And this fruit would never have tempted Eve. Could it?"

"She surely would have wanted to save the tree and see if the fruit didn't improve."

"Adam, of course, would have had to do the work."

"Only if he wanted to."

"He might want simply to please his lady. Even if he knew that she must offer him the fruit, tempt him till he fell—" Angier's tone which had gentled to playfulness grew harsh. "Do you know Scripture, Miss Hastings?

126

The evil tree bears evil fruit."

"You can't neglect an orchard and then call it evil!"

A vein in his forehead throbbed. He gave her an angry stare, then laughed. "One can't let nettles sprout and complain of being stung! All right, Miss Hastings. Shall we make a deal?"

"I'm in no position to bargain with you," she said, hotly aware that he was amused by her.

"Well, let us say that you represent the trees' right to live—my conscience, as it were. That leaves me free to do what I've wanted to once I've satisfied your conditions."

"I'm not sure—"

"Who is? Hush, dear lady, and give ear! I will have the gardeners take off the ivy and get professionals in to prune the orchard after the trees are dormant this fall, and do whatever they judge might help. I won't even expect results this year. But if, a full year after being released from their viney chains, these trees still malinger, bringing forth runty bitter fruit, then down they come!"

"But—"

"No buts! Out of this rather nettle-ridden Eden they shall go! Come, Miss Hastings! Won't you risk a wager?"

"I suppose it's better than leaving the orchard like this," Erica conceded.

"What graciousness!" He chuckled, taking her hand as if to seal the agreement, but holding it longer than necessary. "Cheer up! If these trees go, you shall plant the first tree of a new orchard, I promise!"

Almost two years from now? How could he seem so sure she would still be at Lady Gift?

"Now as to your exercise," he said briskly. "I could

do with some, too. How about a game of tennis each day around three?"

"I don't play well," she evaded.

"All the more exercise for me, then." Without knowing how it had happened, she was moving along with him to the gate. He was in such an agreeable temper that she took a deep breath and plunged.

"Kim is writing a play, Mr. Matthews, and costuming her dolls to act it out. I'm sure it would delight her if you would watch the production."

His smile grew remote but after only a moment's hesitation, he shrugged. "Just say when opening night is."

Braced for a struggle, Erica was thrown off balance by his consent. Why was he so bewildering, warm and friendly one minute, aloof and caustic the next? Whatever his quirks, he was Kim's father, and the more he played that role, the more convincing it would be.

Silence closed on them as they walked along the herbaceous border and across the broad, perfectly kept lawns to the great house. Geraniums and begonias had replaced wallflowers and pansies in the large stone planters beneath each window.

"You can tell the season by whatever flowers are out," Angier said, following her gaze. "Do you know snowdrops, Miss Hastings? They're tiny white flowers that pop up everywhere in February. So do yellow aconites, and then it's not long before primroses carpet beneath the wych elm and chestnuts, and daffodils spring up. These are all wild and the gardeners mow around them. The planted flowers are beautiful, but I like the wild ones—the early ones that fight up through the snow without any help."

"I wouldn't have expected that. With your bent for

perfection, you should prefer cultured rare flowers —orchids, chrysanthemums, dahlias—"

"No doubt. But your relentless logic will lead you into error if you apply it to people!" They paused in the hall near the door that led to the inner court which Erica could not see without remembering Caitlyn. Neither, apparently, could Angier.

"For instance," he mused bitterly, "what makes sense of Caitlyn? I was doing her damn play—could have done it faster without her hovering! She had friends in London, a luxury flat, enough money, and was still a fine actress and stunning woman. What made her jump?"

"Maybe she didn't," said Erica.

She was unprepared for the look that shot across his face. "What do you mean?" he asked.

"What I said—maybe Caitlyn didn't jump."

He caught her wrists in a bruising grip. "Do you know anything I haven't heard? Did you see anything up there—hear anything?"

"No!" She struggled, taking fright. "Why does everyone keep on about it? I just looked over and saw her. That's all I know!"

"I'm sorry." Steadying Erica, he slowly released her. "I'm sure she killed herself. She had tried often enough, God knows! But if there's a chance someone shoved her—if that someone is on the loose at Lady Gift—well, you can understand that I'd be worried!"

Unless it was you, Erica thought, with a thrill of warning. *Then your only fear would be that you might get caught.*

"There is such a thing as a fugue state," Angier went on. "It's a brief amnesia where the person may do all kinds of things he will later not have the faintest

129

memory of. A psychiatrist, Miss Hastings, might sa
you didn't remember everything that happened on th
roof."

"Are you saying—" Erica gazed in shock. "Are yo
hinting that I killed Caitlyn?"

"Of course not! But it's possible that finding he
blotted out anything that happened earlier."

"I'm sure it didn't! I was fixing the ladder, and the
went out to look on the roof. I wasn't in any wa
worried or upset till I saw her!"

"Don't distress yourself, Miss Hastings!" His han
dropped gently, bracingly on her shoulder. "I'm as su
as can be that Caitlyn finally walked off that thin edg
that divides artistic genius and insanity till all tha
mattered to her was revenge of some kind. Poo
beautiful, crazy Cait! All she could hurt with was he
own death! But if you do have any stirrings of memory
however vague, do tell me at once."

He smiled slowly, eyes lingering till in spite o
Erica's troubled anxiety, she had a warming, happ
sense that he cared about and wanted to protect he
"After all," he added, sobering as he turned away
"you might get pushed. If she was killed—and I don'
for an instant believe that—whoever did it might fea
you could incriminate them and try to put you out o
the way. We don't want that!"

Erica certainly didn't!

She almost ran up the stairs. *Study it*, Sybil ha
warned. Erica hated to think about the suicide o
murder, but knew she could not shut her eyes t
something that might cost her own life, or someon
else's. She took off her work clothes, showered, and sa
down at the desk where her thesis lay, but her mind wa
far from the fanciful masques of Inigo Jones.

If Caitlyn's death was not suicide or accident, who caused it? Who would have benefited from it?

Angier obviously would have less emotional and financial pressure; Sybil had been jealous and resentful of the other woman; Malcolm might have his enigmatic reasons; it was even conceivable that Peg had done it to end Caitlyn's urging that Kim be sent to boarding school.

There were other people around Lady Gift, Mrs. Shell, the daily women and the gardeners. Theoretically even Kim was suspect since she used the roof, hated Caitlyn, and had been angry when the actress began to sun there.

Erica's flesh prickled at the hideous thought. Such an encounter would have been accidental. Caitlyn could have made some of her cutting remarks, Kim replied in kind, and if Caitlyn had tried to cuff the child, it was entirely likely that Kim would have dodged, or even retaliated. Kim wouldn't push Caitlyn over on purpose; but it was terrifying clear that could have come about. No one could blame Kim for an accident, but it would be a terrible thing for her to try to hide—

Nonsense! Erica told herself. In a minute she'd begin to think maybe she had been in that fugue state Angier suggested—that maybe she had grappled with Caitlyn and had the memory blotted out by horror!

She switched to another question. Who had the opportunity?

Malcolm claimed an alibi, but no exact time had been given for Caitlyn's death. She had been absent at breakfast and lunch. Any of the possible killers would have had a chance to go to the roof. But who knew that Caitlyn was using it, besides Peg, Kim and Erica?

She probably jumped—or slipped, Erica decided in nervous exhaustion. She tried to sort out her notes on masques, but made little progress. She deliberately thought of Martin, shut her eyes, and discovered between relief and ruefulness, that she could not visualize his smile.

Angier's dark face kept watching her. She felt his hands on her again, the disquieting, piercing awareness of his strength and presence.

He was a playwright. He knew how to produce effects.

Was that fair? He had undertaken a good deal with the orchard. Surely he wouldn't have done that unless he had a genuine desire for her good opinion.

Or unless he wanted to keep her out of it?

Erica weighted down her papers and rose. She was full of morose imaginings and suspicions! It mustn't be allowed. She went in search of Kim, pausing halfway down the stairs to the butler's pantry at a burst of laughter and Kim's shrill delighted giggle threading above the gardeners' husky merriment, as Peg chuckling too, proceeded.

"Now lads—and lassie—as me mother was a lady so she trained me. 'A lady always walks away from an altercation,' she'd say. 'Don't lower yourself by entering into dispute with low characters!' And I try to do as she taught. But that woman bumped me with her backside, she did, and stood there grinning. No pardon or sorry or anything! I looked at her and I thought, 'A lady walks off—but should I let her get away with that and her grinning?' And I got up behind her then, when she wasn't looking—set my backside along hers, I did, and whoosh! Lifted her six feet away. Then I strolled off most unconcerned and ladylike!"

"Taught her a lesson, it must have!" applauded one the men.

"Nice work!" cried another.

Erica retreated up the stairs, called from the top. Kim! Are you down there?"

"Erica!" floated up Kim's clear shriek of pleasure. 'm coming!"

"Don't break your neck on the stairs!" warned Peg, unding none too happy at Kim's ready desertion.

As Kim appeared, puffing, at the top, Erica said, 'm going to the post office and thought you might e to come along and get a popsicle—an ice-lollie," e amended, at Kim's questioning look.

"Super!" cried Kim.

Holding Erica's hand, she chattered at full speed till, unding into the small grocery store adjoining the st office cubicle, she lost herself in choosing between ed creations in a rainbow of brilliant colors.

"I suppose I can't have chocolate," she said, looking stfully at some fudge-covered bars.

"No, and I can't either, or my nose goes blo-o-otch!" m gasped with laughter and Erica said, "Pick what u think is nicest and I'll have one, too."

She paid ninepence each for tri-colored lollies vered with crushed peppermint. "I shall save half of ine in the freezer," decided Kim as they scuffed up e gravel drive. "Oh, I haven't fed the baby mollies ce lunch. Please, Eric, may I run on and do it?"

Erica waved the child on but lingered beside the rved unicorns to finish the sticky ice. She didn't want be seen with it.

Her gaze traveled from the great redwood to the odar, the towering cedar of Lebanon and the uglas fir. How beautiful it was! But very still, almost

133

as if the parklands slept. If there were only som
flowers around the rockery—

Sybil and Angier came around the house. Sybil
arm was looped through his and he had his hand ov
hers in what seemed protective reassurance. She wa
smiling up at him with an adoration that pierced Eric

If Sybil was in fear of her life because of this ma
she hid it extraordinarily well! But she might try
frighten off a competitor; would she kill one?

"Erica!" cried Sybil. "Heavens, an ice-lollie!"

The melting stickiness dripped down Erica's arn
She took an assertive bite of it. "Kim and I have ju
been to the shop."

"Maybe you and I could stroll down, Angier,
suggested Sybil. "I haven't had an ice-lollie since pigta
days! It might be rather fun!"

She might have been talking about an amusin
slightly vulgar heathen rite.

"I think it takes a certain outlook to appreciate ic
lollies," Angier said. "You must show me how one da
Miss Hastings." He nodded pleasantly and opened th
door for Sybil, who went in laughing.

Cheeks burning, Erica finished the ice and used he
handkerchief to open the door. Now Angier woul
think she went about flourishing magenta-lime-orang
lollies! No Englishwoman would. But Kim had enjoye
the sharing so.

Washing vigorously, Erica glimpsed her lolli
colored mouth in the mirror, scrubbed it and manage
a grin. *Easy. Are you working toward a nervo
collapse over a lollie?*

She went into Kim's room, and, while the chil
worked on her play, sewed at King Henry's plume
velvet hat.

"Peg says Angier won't come to my play," Kim said, casting Erica a testing glance, and trying a wistful tune on the flute-like recorder.

"He will," Erica promised.

Easier said—but at least it was comforting in this house of dark riddles to have a clear purpose and solid aims.

XI

The coroner ruled that Caitlyn's death was accidental. No more investigators came to Lady Gift. Angier went up to London for the funeral. There were no more pictures of Caitlyn or Angier in the papers. Below-stairs gossip turned to other things, and Erica found life settling into a routine that was seldom troubled by any lingering doubt about how the actress had died.

Caitlyn had slipped, or at worst jumped. Even Sybil and Malcolm accepted it. Caitlyn had been bent on destruction and consciously or unconsciously had found it.

From breakfast to lunch, there were lessons, with time off for a swim on warm days and half an hour of yoga. After lunch Peg took charge of Kim for a few hours, giving Erica some time for her own affairs, including half an hour's tennis most days with Angier.

He liked tea immediately afterward and Erica had learned to make it, taking the "kettle to the pot" at high boil. They would talk, mostly about Kim or plays, for precisely fifteen minutes, when Angier would glance at his watch and Erica, faintly annoyed, would collect the tea things and leave his suite. At least he had encouraged her to do over Kim's room, and Erica gradually, with Kim's agreement, began making the child's room bright and suitable for a young girl.

Erica had found a Latin dictionary and now that she had her English driver's license some afternoons she drove with Kim to the cathedral or a church in some nearby village where they would decipher inscriptions. Kim amassed a variety of quotes which she rolled out at the slenderest excuse. "*Da quod iubes, et iube quod vis,*" she was fond of saying when Erica besought her to try to remember her multiplication tables. "Give what you command and command what you will." Or, when Angier inquired after her progress in a subject: "*'Ignoramus sed non ignorabimus.'* That means, Father, that we don't know, but we will!"

"Mmmm," smiled Angier, rubbing his chin and looking over Kim's head to Erica. "What does that leave me to say except *'Quod enim malvult homo verum esse, id potius credit.'* What a man would rather were true, he easily believes!"

Angier had dinner with the household most of the time. He seemed less stiff with Kim and often looked directly at her instead of past.

"Don't you feel like a patriarch, Angier?" asked Malcolm one evening. "Of course it really needs a few more children, and your hair's not white."

"Give it time," Angier grinned equably.

"It's nice to have you with us," Sybil murmured. She evidently believed his presence was due to the absence of Caitlyn, and in her chair opposite Angier she rang the bell for courses and generally acted as mistress of the house.

After all, she once had been.

Angier agreed to attend Kim's premiere. Taking their cue from the master, Sybil and Malcolm came, too, and Peg asked diffidently if she might watch.

137

Mrs. Shell and Erica made up the group that met in the library to watch Kim manipulate a resplendent Henry the Eighth through his struggles to be rid of Katherine of Aragon, marry Anne, and in turn be rid of her.

As the doll dressed in Anne's prison robe had its stiff little arm brought up to its throat and Kim whispered dramatically, "I have such a little neck!" Erica saw Angier's almost rapt attention. But then Kim, stealing a glance at her audience, and apparently unwilling to lose their attention, picked up another girl doll and led directly into Henry's adventure with Jane Seymour.

She dawdled, paused to think, and was plainly making up the action and dialogue on the spot. Sybil yawned. Malcolm moved restively and a frown began and grew on Angier's face. Peg and Mrs. Shell still watched dotingly as Kim wrestled on, and Erica wondered how to end the performance without spoiling the child's triumph.

Poor Jane Seymour's life had ended so soon that this episode couldn't last long. Erica resolved to start clapping at poor Jane's last breath and get Kim off stage, or off table, since the play was being acted out on the polished refectory board.

"That's enough, Kim," Angier said, as he rose to his feet. "The first part of the play was very well done. But an actor or playwright cannot expect an audience to sit through rehearsal." He looked at Sybil, who was smiling cozily up at him. "Let's give our performer an ovation for her excellent story of Anne Boleyn!"

Everyone clapped, but Kim, whose big eyes growing bigger at his every word had been fixed on her father, dropped her splendidly robed dolls and fled.

"Kim!" Angier shouted, but she ran on, head ducked

into the bend of her elbow. Peg shot Angier a lowering angry look and followed.

"Little too professional, weren't you, Angier, for a first performance?" asked Malcolm, in his detached way.

"She has to learn," retorted Sybil.

Erica, numbed, picked up the dolls. What should have been Kim's triumph had turned to humiliation; what should have created a bond between father and daughter had created a wound— Erica blinked back tears of furious hurt and made for the door.

It closed. Angier blocked her way.

"Hastily hasten not hence, Miss Hastings!" His rich voice made a mocking, hateful litany. "I suppose you think me a low dog, a Herod—"

"The slaughter of the innocent is apt enough!" Erica flamed. "Talk about overkill—"

She reached for the doorknob. His long, lean fingers closed over hers.

"Erica—"

"No!" she cried, wresting open the door.

She ran upstairs, heard Peg's soothing croon above the sound of hiccupy weeping. "There, poppet, it was a grand play! So real and all! It was clever of you to make up the speeches and remember them! Would you want to finish off the bloody old king now? I'll watch!"

"Angier didn't like it, Peg! He was b-b-bored!"

"Couldn't have been, poppet! But you know how he is about time—can't stand to lose a second."

"He was bored all the time!" Kim wailed. "He thought my play was silly!"

Peg muttered something indistinct. "There, there, my lamb," she said. Erica knocked and entered Kim's room with the dolls.

"You did very well," she told Kim. "If you polish up the rest of the story, I'm sure we could have another theatre night."

"I don't want to," Kim drooped, eyes red and swollen.

Peg said with heavy humor, "Your pa's just jealous, Kimmie! Sees his competition budding out!"

"I don't want to make up any more plays." The child's face looked as grimly set as Angier's could on occasion.

"I hope you'll change your mind," Erica said. "But anyway it's time to tuck in. Go have your shower."

"Shall Peg sleep by your door tonight, poppet?" asked the big girl.

"No, thank you, Peg," said Kim, frighteningly composed after her storm. "I'm not afraid now that Erica's here." The girl slid out of Peg's ample embrace and in a moment the shower started running.

Peg gave Erica a look that was freezing in its hatred. "Will you credit that? The lamb not afraid with *you* here! When you let her in for that shame she had from Lord High and Mighty!"

"I'm sorry it went sour." Erica's cheeks burned and she couldn't keep defensive note out of her voice. "It seemed a way to get them together. I thought Kim's father would be very proud of her. And he was, till she started inventing."

"You cannot make that man have a heart, not him, the devil!" Peg nearly raged. "Oh, he wants the child around, it's all of her mother he has, but then he takes out on Kimmie that the poor lady's dead! If you care for the child, keep her shut of that ice-blooded creature, don't put her in the way of him!"

Peg went off, shoulders squared, hips plumping.

Erica, completely dashed, worried over Kim, and hotly resentful of Angier, went into her bedroom and made up Kim's nest on the chaise. When Kim came in, smelling of perfumed soap and wearing her new pajamas, she lay down and listened to Erica read from the *Chronicles of Narnia* for the half hour that had become their custom, but she dropped into sleep, or pretended to, before Erica noticed.

Putting down the book of sorceresses, singing lions and dying moons, Erica spread the sheet more evenly over Kim, so strikingly beautiful with her long hair spangling the pillow, long, dark lashes above flushed cheeks and her mouth like a down-curving wing.

How could Angier be so hard with her?

Erica tried to read for her thesis, but kept seeing Kim's stricken face, hearing Angier's cutting rebuke to Kim, the spiteful anger in Peg's accusation.

She had meant to waken Angier to his child; instead she had brought the thunderbolt of his disapproval down on Kim, who could be irksome, single-minded to a nerve-fraying degree, but was of a nature open, eager and loving.

Erica could not concentrate and it was too early for bed. She closed her book, slipped into a warm Arran cardigan, shut her door quietly, and went down the gallery in a way that could only be described as stealthy. Going out by the sunroom's French doors seemed the least likely way to rouse anyone.

Down the stairs past the pleading hands, through the lower hall, where a wall sconce always shone at night, into the room now lighted not by the sun but by a full silver moon casting patches on the straw matting.

Finding the large ornate key in the lock, Erica turned it, and stepped into the night, locking the door on the outside and slipping the key into her cardigan pocket.

It was so light that the cedar of Lebanon cast a great splotch of shadow toward the sundial. The Douglas fir loomed like a giant monster and the little wych elm rustled demurely in the western breeze. Erica turned along the herbaceous border, caught the sweet smell of lilies high as her shoulder, smiled at the white Michaelmas daisies, drank in the fragrance of hundreds of roses, and opened the iron gate that led through the walled garden.

Broad beans, peas, onions and carrots looked in the ghostly light like mysterious plants from a witch's furrows, but there was rich strong reality in the smell of freshly turned loam. The new trees at the lower part of the enclosure bore fruit that looked silver or luminous blue-green.

The enchanted hush seemed to deepen when Erica opened the next gate and stood in the Old Orchard. She had not been here since the day Angier had in one breath commanded her to stop her rescue operations and promised to have the trees looked after.

He had kept his word, with a not altogether pleasing result, for where vines had been stripped away, knotted tumors gave the trees a grotesque look. A few trees which had been choked to splayed stubs of trunk and bough looked like upstretched hands with their fingers mutilated. Erica touched one pityingly.

But surely in a season or two fresh growth would cover the scars, and though the decades-old trunk deformities might not change much, the trees could live and bear good fruit again.

Nettles and weeds had been cleared from the center of the orchard except for a small patch in the very middle. Erica moved toward it and found a young acacia grown about by briars and convolvulus that nearly hid several white stone markers.

Tombstones!

Chilled, Erica bent to try to make out the lettering on the nearest one. There was a single name, nearly obscured, with dates beneath, 1900-1903—before Angier's time.

With considerable relief, Erica reflected that this was an odd place for a child to be buried. The dates on the next stone indicated a life span of eight years, the next of ten, and on this one the name was clearly legible: *Springer*.

"It's the pet cemetery."

She whirled to find Angier so close that she stepped back. "Oh!" she gasped, feeling guilty and foolish. "I—I didn't hear you."

Was his laugh strange or did she imagine it? "It's scarcely the time or place to expect to meet anyone—unless you've made a lover's tryst in my orchard, Miss Hastings. But such a proper young lady wouldn't do such a thing, would she?"

"I—just wanted to take a walk," Erica said stiffly.

"Quite."

He showed no sign of moving. Erica moved sideways to the briars. "I'd better be going on," she stammered. "Good night."

Her foot caught in a convolvulus tangle. She pitched forward, would have fallen except for Angier's hands which checked her fall, brought her around facing him.

"Don't run off. I was restless, too—a result of my behavior at the play which I shall explain in a moment! Tell me, Miss Hastings—Erica—did you come to see if that beastly, insufferable man had at least kept his word about clearing the orchard?"

He still held her arms. A warm, weakening feeling spread through Erica. Suspicious as she sometimes was of Angier, angry as she still was, she could not pretend to herself any longer that she was not vitally attracted to this moody, imperious man.

"I wanted to walk someplace," she evaded.

He laughed tenderly, chidingly. "And of course there aren't twenty acres of Lady Gift! No, Erica, you came to see what I'd done to the orchard." His tone changed and his grip tightened. "When you saw the stones, what did you think? That I'm a Bluebeard who buries pretty girls among the nettles?"

"I—I didn't think anything! I was just curious!"

"Fabled last excuses," he said lightly.

He was not exerting pressure but she was quite helpless in his grasp. "Let's find a bench," he suggested. "Let me tell you why I took a tough approach to Kim this evening, and then if you'll forgive my sternness, I'll overlook your curiosity so long as it doesn't develop to the 'satiable enormity of Kipling's elephant's child!"

They went back the way she had come. He kept his hand under her arm till they were crossing the broad lawns by the huge trees, and then he took her hand, drew her to a stone bench near the sundial.

"A moondial tonight," he said. "The moon's a fairy godmother to all us Cinderellas, it changes us, hides a lot and softens the rest." He leaned forward in mock-serious scrutiny. "You are always a joy to behold, Miss Hastings, and in this light you are bewitching!"

Her heart leaped and then began to beat so fast that she thought he must hear it or feel the speeding pulse in her wrist.

"That sounds like dialogue from a script," she said,

forcing coolness into her voice. "Do you want to find out if it plays well?"

He frowned a bit, then shrugged. "Does it?"

This sweetly delicious, frightening effect he had on her! Erica struggled for composure, tried to summon Martin's face and got only a vague outline. He was a dim shadow of recollection. But Angier—Angier had captured her thoughts and longings as securely as he now had her hands.

"The dialogue is most—effective," she managed to say lightly.

"Good. Then perhaps I can venture to make you understand why I couldn't let Kim drag out her performance. You seem to doubt that!" he teased, as Erica looked away, distress over the child quenching much of her excited pleasure.

"Kim was so thrilled to have you there, and she had worked very hard—"

"Not hard enough! Or rather, she tried to stretch her act beyond her preparation!"

"But surely it wasn't all that important!"

Angier's jaw hardened. "For most children, maybe not. An hour's occasional boredom is a cost of parenthood, I suppose. I was not being the cruel father smashing toys, Erica. Kim has great talent. I've never glimpsed it before." He laughed stumblingly. "That means, you are surely saying to yourself in that prim decisive way you have, that I've never watched her closely or long enough to recognize her qualities. I can only hope you will believe that it can be too painful to look, too painful to see."

And remember? wondered Erica with a stab of pain. Was the mother so like Kim?

"If I have learned anything in twenty years of

writing plays and seeing stage people flash and fade, it's that there's much more talent than there is discipline and perseverance." Angier's firm grip compelled her to listen. "Kim has a flair for dialogue and phrasing—that came through, even when the brat ad-libbed! I think she could do anything in the theater—act, write, direct, produce—if she will get a foundation before she tries to build. But if our Kim's not guided, she'll bluff, dash and helter-skelter, wasting her brilliance."

"Good heaven! You're speaking of a nine-year-old!"

"I'm speaking of an agile mind that knew very well it was trying to pull a fast one. With luck, it won't need another lesson."

"It may not!" flashed Erica. "Kim says she doesn't want to do any more plays."

Angier rocked back, relaxing his hold. After a moment he said, "Childish temper!"

"As you said, Kim's far from a usual child."

"She couldn't have worked up that little drama unless it was really in her blood," he said confidently. When Erica didn't smile or look at him, he got abruptly to his feet. "If it does stifle her stage aims, I can be sure that I've saved her a lot of grief."

"By causing it now?"

He turned as if stung by an unseen whip. "I've seen Kim's temperament and where it leads, unless it's disciplined! Don't presume to lecture me about my child, Miss Hastings! God knows she's all I have left!" He spun on his heel, called over his shoulder, "It's time you came in. I don't like the feel of someone of the household out wandering this late."

Was this the man who had paid her compliments, held her hands, seemed eager for her good opinion?

146

Tears smarted as Erica sprang up and went past him with her head high.

"Wait!" he called.

Let him see she was crying? Erica ran into the house, shut the French doors, and locked them in his face, which stared through the glass first in bewilderment, then anger, then startled amusement as she whirled away.

She heard his laughter and then, as she fled upstairs, she heard the click of a key and the opening of a door.

XII

Angier didn't come to dinner the next few evenings, which was probably fortunate since Kim, ordinarily sweet-tempered and puppily enthusiastic, was sunk in a silence broken only by barbed remarks. She was clearly on her dignity after public humiliation and her kitten's claws, once unfurled, displayed accuracy and the ability to wound.

"Angier must be terribly busy on his play," Sybil remarked anxiously at lunch the second day his place was empty. "He hasn't even dictated letters yesterday or this morning."

Erica wondered if he were vexed with her, ashamed of his harshness with Kim, or simply bored with them all.

"Her master's voice!" scoffed Kim.

"Don't be cheeky!" Sybil ordered, flushing.

"Well, you have seen ads with that dog cocking its head toward a gramophone—"

Erica touched the child's shoulder, said quietly, "Kim."

Kim shot her a bright arrogant look but she addressed herself to kippers instead of Sybil before she finished and ran off.

When Erica moved down the gallery, she heard Peg's voice coming from Kim's room. "Yes, poppet, me great-grandmother had a son by the lord, she did, and his lordship took the boy, raised him and sent him to fancy schools. Did handsome by my great-gran, too, married her to a farmer and gave them a cottage on the estate. He must of fancied my great-gran!"

Fascinated by this bit of living folklore, Erica stopped in the hall. It wasn't *really* eavesdropping when they left a door open.

"What happened to the son?" demanded Kim.

"He went to Australia, had an enormous sheep station, got richer than his lordship, and popped off with apoplexy at a horse race," recounted Peg. "Gran should have inherited from him, of course, since he died a bachelor, but he'd been given his father's name and there was no way of proving my family were true kin. Otherwise," dreamed Peg, "I'd be a fine lady and have a maid instead of being one."

Kim snorted. "You act proud to have a bastard in the family!"

"Bastard!" screeched Peg after a minute of shock. "He were a lord's son, ye wee baggage!"

"He was still a—"

"Kim!" called Erica. "Where are you?"

"Here!" Kim tumbled out of her room. She looked glad to escape but was checked by the look on Erica's face. "Come in my room, please," Erica said.

Head down, casting looks between entreaty and defiance, Kim followed. "Now," said Erica, shutting the door. "What's the matter? You were rude to Sybil, but you hurt Peg, who is your friend."

"That boy was a bastard!"

"That's a rather stupid classification that shouldn't mean more than being right- or left-handed. Anyway, we're not concerned with that. Why hurt Peg?"

"I—I—" Kim's lip trembled. Tears gathered in her

149

eyes and Erica had to steel herself to keep from catching the child close and comforting her. "I feel all tight and prickly!" Kim burst out. "People just talk, talk, looking smug, and nobody says anything to them, but they say what they like to me! If—if I told Angie one of his plays wasn't any good—"

"He didn't say your play wasn't good," Erica pointed out. "He recognized when you went past what you had rehearsed." Kim looked sulky and unconvinced. "Shall I tell you what he told me?" Erica asked.

"He—he talked about my play?" In spite of herself, Kim turned eager, flung her arms around Erica. "Oh, Eric, what did he say?"

"He said your play was extremely good but that you would have to learn to rehearse and practice and work over something before you could make a performance of it. He was hard on you, Kim, *because* he thought it was so good."

"Truly?"

"Truly!"

Kim hugged Erica tight, recoiled in sudden doubt. "You wouldn't say that to make me feel better?"

"No." Erica laughed. "I wouldn't even say it to make you act better!"

Still in Erica's arms, Kim said reflectively after a few rapt moments, "Actually, I have been thinking about a play, rather. One about Lady Margaret and her Cornish gentleman."

"Work it up," Erica counseled briskly. "Now hadn't you better find Peg and tell her you're sorry?"

Kim grimaced. "I don't have to tell her, do I? I can just go up and give her a kiss. She won't stay off-put—"

"You hurt her with words. Don't you think you

150

should find words to make it right?"

"Mmm." Kim glanced up, saw no hint of relenting, and sighed. "All right!" She went out, the familiar buoyancy restored to her skipping walk.

Erica's heart felt lighter than it had since the night of the play. Kim, as Angier had predicted, had drama in her blood, she wouldn't be quenched easily. But couldn't she turn spiteful, the little witch!

Now, if Angier would come out of his seclusion — Could he be in a temper over her locking the door in his face? Erica insisted to herself that she didn't care. It was none of his business how long she walked in the moonlight! Yet she drew a ridiculous amount of reassurance from remembering that after she had locked the door, he *had* laughed.

Kim bounced back to high spirits with alarming vigor, shouting to Peg across the formerly sacrosanct gallery, singing ballads and Beatle music off key, and never walking when she could run. Candy wrappers and ice-lollie sticks appeared outside the kitchen and her room.

"She acts like one of the village children!" observed Mrs. Shell, in a tone hovering between horror and approval. "Do American children fly about like that, Miss Hastings?"

"You should have known some of my pupils," Erica laughed. "I suppose Kim should be a little quieter, though."

"My dear Lord, no! Leave her be! This gloomy old place needs lighting up and children be the best lamps, don't they, bobbing around as they do? Pity there aren't half a dozen!"

151

Was the housekeeper's alert blue eye inquisitive? Erica smiled. "I don't think even Lady Gift could hold six like Kim!"

"She's got a light heart and step, just like her mother, but bringing this place to life—well, it takes more than one to do it!" Mrs. Shell polished the already gleaming sixteenth-century chest on the landing. "Mr. Angier, he knows it! He's always telling me to leave a few of the child's books lying about, says they give the rooms a lived-in look! I say expecting any child, alone, to brighten Lady Gift is like turning a firefly loose in a dungeon!"

"I suppose it doesn't matter so long as Kim doesn't feel it's dark," said Erica.

She was moving along the gallery, past Mrs. Shell's "Humph!" when, from the library, she heard Angier's voice—for the first time since the night in the orchard.

"Kim! What's the sticky mess all over this chair?"

With a sinking feeling, Erica heard Kim's inaudible mumble and Angier's disgusted, "An ice-lollie? You sat reading in this library with one of those disgusting things melting over you, the chair, and probably the book?"

Halfway down the stairs, Erica heard Kim's tremulous voice say, "I didn't mean to, Angier! I—I'll clean it up!"

"I should hope so!"

He came striding out, scowling, tagged by a chastized Kim, and stopped as he saw Erica.

"I trust you will teach Kim where and when ice-lollies are permissible," he said crisply, and went past without another word, though it was the first time Erica had seen him in over a week.

Cheeks flaming, Erica bit back an instinctive retort,

dropped a hand to Kim's shoulder. "Let's clean up the scene of the crime," she said, trying to joke.

"It's melted lollie, not blood," hissed Kim delightedly, as Erica damped a cloth in the nearest bathroom.

"Maybe it's dragon blood," Erica proposed, prying up the leather cushion while Kim scrubbed. "Or it may have come from a unicorn's veins, or perhaps a mermaid flapped in here and ate sea-weed ice cream."

Kim finished the task and looked at Erica with sparkling eyes. "I know why I like you, Eric! You haven't grown up! I mean, you can still pretend—play inside your mind the way I do!"

"I didn't till I met you," Erica said truthfully, with a yearning flash of compassionate sorrow for her mother, who had found some peace in making forms of the creatures in her brain but had finally smashed them. "But I like to pretend with you, Kim. Are you almost through with your play about Lady Margaret?"

Kim nodded. "I can use the same costumes I did for Anne Boleyn, and I've got a thrilling ending! Rehearsed, too!" she added hastily.

"Good. Want a dress rehearsal first with just me?"

"No," decided Kim. "I want everybody to see it at the same time."

"When will it be ready?"

"I was going to ask Angier if he could watch tonight." They had reached the top of the stairs. Kim looked hesitantly toward Angier's door.

The idea! A child being worried about asking her father something, wondering what would happen if she knocked on his door! Erica took Kim's hand.

"Let's find out now," she said briskly, and gave his door as thunderous a rap as she could manage.

The door opened so quickly that she stumbled forward, narrowly avoiding a bump with Angier. "We've come to see if you'll watch Kim's new play tonight," Erica blurted, involuntarily rubbing her smarting knuckles.

Angier raised an eyebrow at his daughter. "A new play? So soon?"

"It's all rehearsed, Angier!"

"You'll be the envy of the Haymarket!" he mused. "I'll come gladly—but let's have this understood: no garbling speeches and chewing the scenery. When you're through with what you've practiced, stop!"

"I will," Kim said, like a knight accepting a quest.

"Good!"

Before anyone guessed what he was doing, he bent to kiss his daughter's forehead. Kim floated out of the room as if walking on a golden cloud. As the door closed behind them, Kim stopped and looked up at Erica.

"He—kissed me!" Her fingers went to the spot his lips had brushed. "Angier kissed me!"

"Fathers do kiss daughters," Erica teased.

Kim shook her head. "Angier never kissed me before!"

"You've just forgotten!"

"I couldn't forget," Kim said positively, as they stopped beside her door. "I'd better practice a little more, just to be sure Lady Margaret remembers all her lines."

"Splendid. I'll be in my room when you're through."

Shaken, Erica went into the rose-and-silver chamber, absentmindedly fondled the unicorn her mother had made during those happy, productive months. Imagine a nine-year-old who couldn't remember having been kissed by her father!

But at least he had done it, and consented with good grace to attend the play.

Erica put down the unicorn and began to write her mother one of those strange letters which might never be read, or if it was, might be twisted and changed by the poor tortured mind attempting to understand it.

Erica labored for an hour on the difficult message, sealed it in an envelope, and called, "Kim! Will you go to the post office with me?"

No answer. Erica went along the gallery and peered in Kim's room. Costumed dolls lay in a heap, but their owner was gone.

Probably she had asked Peg to go for a late swim. Or there was the library. Erica hurried downstairs, circled all the common rooms, but saw no one. She began to feel a bit uneasy though she told herself Kim was surely with Peg. Lady Gift was so big that it was a marvel Kim didn't drop out of sight far oftener than she did.

Just to be thorough, Erica cut through the cellars and entered the butler's pantry. No one was there.

"Peg!"

The lower part, including the venison room, was deserted. Erica went through the courtyard toward the pool, encouraged by the sound of splashing.

Malcolm, doing a fast economical crawl, sighted Erica and waved. "Am I so lucky?" he demanded, levering himself up on the tiles. "Are you coming for a dip?"

"Not now, thanks. Have you seen Kim?"

"Not since lunch."

"Oh. Well, if you do, please tell her to stay in her room till I've seen her."

Malcolm, bronze hair shading into bronze skin, had

155

more than ever his look of handsome falcon. "You're not worried?" he asked with quick concern. "She can't have been gone long."

"No, it's just that I can't find her. I'm sure she's somewhere about."

"Lady Gift has plenty of nooks and crannies. Kim knows them all. Why don't you just wait an hour or so? She'll turn up!"

"I'm sure she will, but—"

"You might go by the Clock House and see if she's visiting Peg's flat or chatting with the gardeners," suggested Malcolm. "If she's not there, let me know and I'll help you track her down."

"That's nice of you," Erica said. It was, especially since he plainly thought she was upset for no reason. But it wasn't like Kim, to vanish without warning.

Erica rang unavailingly at Peg's flat till Mrs. Shell poked her head out of a window and called, "She's gone to town on the bus, Miss Hastings."

"Kim wasn't with her?"

"No, Miss."

Peg had been the best hope. Dashed, Erica fought a tightness in her throat. "You haven't seen Kim?"

"Not since lunch, Miss. Scolded her a bit, I did, for leaving her nice runner beans."

"If you see her, will you send her to the house and tell her to wait for me?" asked Erica.

"To be sure I will, Miss. Don't worry, she'll be somewhere about."

As Erica circled the Clock House, spotting all the gardeners at work with no small figure alongside, she saw a wilting flower dropped on the grass. She knelt to pick it up. Anyone could have dropped it, of course, but Kim was so fond of gathering bouquets.

"No luck?" asked Malcolm, dressed in shorts and shirt.

Erica shook her head, rising, still holding the faded blossom. There was a strange expression in Malcolm's eyes, and a curious little smile played around his long mouth.

"Poor Demeter! Do you think someone from the underground has ravished away your daughter?"

"I suppose it's silly," Erica admitted, "but I am worried. Will you help me look?"

He bowed. "Gladly, though nothing would amuse our little friend more than to see us in a tizzy like this while she's doubtless curled away with a book. Have you looked under the wych elm and that remarkable Douglas fir?"

"I haven't, but I will." Erica took heart. It was a hot day and either tree gave lovely deep shade.

"Good. You look there and then pop into the house to see if she's there. Probably she is. I'll go through the old orchard and down to the village. Perhaps Kimberley decided to go for an ice-lollie on her own." He laughed. "Someday you must let me take you for one!"

"You're very kind," Erica said.

Though her anxiety was heightened in one way, Malcolm's help eased some of her dreadful, nameless fears. She remembered how once she had stopped to play at a friend's on the way from school and how her mother had been frantic when she had finally come innocently home. Neighbors had been searching, and in ten more minutes her mother was going to call the police. Surely there was some similar explanation of Kim's absence.

But she had no playmates, no friends in the village.

157

Lady Gift was a little island, a small kingdom quite separated from the village.

Erica cut back through the walled garden, calling Kim's name. She went to the Douglas fir and shouted. No answer. And none came from the dainty little wych elm.

The house, Malcolm had suggested. Kim must be there by now. Erica ran across the lawns and walks, past the unicorns, and into the main hall. She felt like calling out at once but feared to disturb Angier over what was probably nothing. Running up the stairs, she raced to Kim's room, sickened as she saw it just as it had been.

"Kim!" she called softly, in case the child was in her bathroom.

Next she went along to her own room. It was empty, too. Suddenly, Erica could stand it no longer. "Kim!" she cried. Her voice flared, broke, rose out of control, and she found herself gripping the gallery rail, shouting through the silent, echoing house.

"Kim! Kim! Kim!"

XIII

Angier came out of his room, looking tousled, and as he said, "What's wrong?" Erica remembered the first night she had come to this house and his grudging interview. Would it have been better for everyone, including the child who was lost, if she, Erica, had never entered Lady Gift? Kim's voice, from the tree, had been the first one she had heard there.

Now, watching Angier as he came along the gallery, Erica said, "I can't find Kim."

"Can't find her?" His face darkened. "Has she been gone long?"

"She wanted to rehearse her play on her own. I went to my room and told her to come in when she was through. When she didn't after an hour, I looked and found her gone."

Angier shrugged. "She's probably with Peg."

Did he think she, Erica, would start shouting through the house unless she had some reason? "Peg's gone to town alone. Mrs. Shell hasn't seen Kim, nor has Malcolm, who's hunting in the orchard and village. I did find a flower she could have dropped." Erica held it out. It was as if, till Kim appeared, she had to keep this possible vestige of her.

Angier had already looked weary, but he grew haggard almost before Erica's eyes. "How long have you been hunting? Where have you been?"

"The library, the kitchen where they used to cut up the game and fowl, the air raid shelter and summer pavilion, the walled garden, the wych elm and Douglas fir, the swimming pool and Clock House—"

It was almost a list of the places Kim had shown her their first day together. Time—the past—it seemed one should be able to step back into it, especially at Lady Gift, where Angier's past, embodied in people, existed around him while the sundial marked the hour. . . .

I have to get away from here! Erica thought in a wave of panic. *I hate it, so dark and big and sad. It's a tomb! Everyone here is smothered or dying or dead!*

Yet Kim lived in this past-haunted house. Kim, who must be found! And Erica knew she could never leave the child—and did not want to leave this tall, strange man who watched her from across the gallery.

"She must be around!" he said. "Maybe she's sulking because I ticked her off about having ice-lollies in the library."

"She's not sulking." Anger burned through Erica's anxiety. She stared at him, determined to make him see himself if it cost her job, and spoke in a trembling voice. "Kim is the only life in this place and life has its dripping popsicles and scuffing feet! It makes a mess—it doesn't just leave a few books scattered about for an air of warmth! You crave life—you must, or you wouldn't keep it around you by way of Kim. Yet you chill and crush and quench her till it's a miracle she can still laugh!"

"I'm a monster, am I? The hundred-headed dog of hell or old Pluto himself?"

"There's no use in having a row." As he swiftly approached, she retreated along the gallery. "We have to find Kim!"

Silence hung thick and breathless between them. "We'll discuss these interesting observations of yours later," he said drily. "Have you looked on the sun roof?"

"The roof?" Erica had not even thought of it. After Caitlyn's death, it seemed no one would feel like using it. "Let's see," Angier urged, already moving down the hall.

Fresh energy was in his stride. He went up the ladder ahead of Erica. "Out of deference to your skirts," he said, giving her a hand up, but hurrying along the catwalk.

He must love the child! Erica began to feel ashamed of her tirade and wish she had found a gentler way to point out the same things. In this search for Kim, she felt close, united with Angier.

The window gaped open. Angier, peering through, turned to Erica with a smile and a finger to his lips.

Kim lay sleeping by the chimney, face nestled in the crook of her arm, the slim, curveless yet exquisitely proportioned young body bathed in a light that made her skin translucent.

Angier moved noiselessly onto the roof. It was astonishing that such a big man could keep from making any sound as he crossed to his daughter. Did it trouble him to remember how Caitlyn had fallen, leaped, or been shoved from here?

He bent down. For the second time that day—and in his life, if Kim's memory was accurate, he kissed her.

"Wake up, Sleeping Beauty!"

She smiled, opening her arms even before she opened her eyes. "Angier!" She gave him an ecstatic hug, rubbed her eyes and blinked at Erica. "What are you doing up here?"

"We might ask you that," Angier chuckled, hoisting her up and steering her to the window. He didn't glance at the inner well. "You've been the object of quite a hunt! I guess you'd be in for bread and water if we weren't so relieved. Right, Miss Hastings?"

Glad that he was behaving like this, shaky from relaxed tension, Erica felt a bit like the boy who shouted "Wolf!" "I thought you were coming to my room after your practice," she said to Kim, less in reproach than to verify that fact for Angier.

"I did peek," said Kim. "But you were writing a letter and looked so—sad, rather—that I thought I'd go up on the roof awhile. I didn't mean to go to sleep. Was I there long?"

"I've been hunting you for an hour," Erica said.

"Goodness gracious! I'm sorry, Eric!"

"All's well that ends well," said Angier. "But in future be sure Miss Hastings knows where you are, and don't go up on that roof alone, Kim."

"Are you afraid Lady Margaret might push me?" asked Kim, her bright head level with his elbow as they moved down the gallery.

"Is Peg filling your head with ghosts and nonsense?" he asked sharply. "I've warned her about that."

"Don't be mad with her, Angier," pleaded Kim. "I like to hear all the stories when she's telling them. It's just later I get scared."

"I leave the matter to Miss Hastings," he said. "And now, ladies, goodbye until dinner and the premiere!" He bowed with a flourish and turned into his suite.

"We've got to find Malcolm and tell him he can stop looking for you," Erica told Kim, turning down the stairs.

Kim's eyes sparkled and she danced ahead. "It really

162

was a search! And I had to be asleep and not even know!"

"Don't get notions about doing it on purpose and hiding someplace to watch the show," Erica said dourly.

They found Malcolm at the edge of the village, returning from his fruitless quest. "So, Kimberley," he said in solemn tones after hearing their story, "you were basking in the sun whilst we scoured the environs."

"Quite," she replied with equal gravity.

"It is not the equivalent of a bona fide return of a prodigal," he mused. "So slaughter of a fatted calf would be excessive. But I will stand treat to ice-lollies and ice cream."

"Super!" thrilled Kim. She skipped on ahead toward the shop.

"Remarkable that she would go up on the roof," drawled Malcolm.

"She likes it there."

"But after poor dear Cait—" Erica said nothing. Malcolm shrugged. "Maybe I shouldn't say this, Erica, but I'm too fond of you to care to see your remains at the bottom of the well. Don't go up on that roof alone—or with Kim and Peg. Especially not with them."

"What do you mean?"

Malcolm spoke painfully as if he had to force out each word. "I hate to even think of it—but Kimberley worships Angier. She doesn't want to see him marry. He pays her pitifully little attention as it is and any fool could see that he's more than slightly intrigued with you. She loathed Caitlyn—with reason, be it admitted. And Peg—well, Peg is afraid of any competing power

163

that lessens her ferociously possessive grip on the child."

"You've lived in a playwright's house too long," scoffed Erica in spite of her prickling scalp.

He shrugged. "Maybe. But someone pushed Cait. Why don't you leave while you can?" His hazel eyes went over her so that she blushed. "Lady Gift has a way of proving fatal for lovely young women."

"Sybil hasn't died."

He laughed. "Sybil has worn extremely well—still she is neither young nor lovely. You are."

"You have a way of paying compliments that makes me wish you wouldn't!"

Malcolm laughed, crooned in her ear as he opened the shop door: "I did but see her passing by, and yet I love her till she die. . . ." With a glint in his hazel eyes, he gestured toward the freezer. "What will you have, my lady? Step right up and name your poison!"

"That's not an inviting way of putting it!"

"Sorry," he twinkled. "Thought my western barkeep terminology would make you feel at home. Ice-lollie, Kim?"

Erica chose vanilla Cornish, wished she could thank Malcolm for it with more graciousness. Why was he such an *uncomfortable* person, prying up things best left hidden? Kim wouldn't hurt anyone, but Peg—

Oh, it was nonsense, all of it! Caitlyn had slipped or fallen!

The same group that had watched the first play assembled in the library for Kim's new presentation. She played her recorder as they got settled, an Elizabethan-sounding medley lilting with *Greensleeves,* that ended on a drawn-out note, and began

164

what she proclaimed as "The Tragical Story of Lady Margaret."

The velvet-and-sable-clad Lady was shown entering the dower house as a happy bride with her gallant husband. She was even happier singing lullabies to a baby while the dark gentleman from Cornwall looked on, first with pride, then with suspicion, till the day he confronted her with his jealous accusations and the sword that lopped off her beautiful hands.

The young producer portrayed this by spurting catsup which covered what seemed the stubs of wrists, a harrowing shriek, and the dropping to the table of tiny pink hands.

"Made 'em of marzipan, I did!" giggled Peg.

The husband fled, cursing in Spanish that sounded more like Latin mottoes, while the old nurse wept over her dying mistress and promised to raise the baby.

In the last act, Kim brought out a doll-sized replica of the stairs and banister carved with hands, leading up to a landing where the Lady stood with her bloody handless arms outstretched, stalking an unsuspecting woman dressed in a flame bikini. It could only represent Caitlyn. The Lady shoved Caitlyn, who fell and lay in a crumpled heap as the Lady moved slowly down the staircase and Kim held the recorder with her free hand and sang between mournful notes:

> "If ever you feel hands at your back,
>   It's Margaret, Margaret!
> If ever you feel tears on your cheek,
>   It's Margaret, Margaret!
> And the sigh on the stairs
> And the crying wind
> Is Margaret's grief that can never end

Till she finds her hands and her baby son
She must walk this house, poor ghostly one!"

In spite of lugubrious touches like the catsup and marzipan hands, Erica felt touches of chill and real involvement throughout the drama. The recorder music and the weird little song were hauntingly right for the story. She only wished, as she joined the clapping led by Angier, that Kim had not brought in Caitlyn's death.

Kim, flushed with triumph, made the dolls dip and bow to the applause, gaze fixed on her father.

"Well done!" he told her. "As Shakespeare might have said, 'Excellent well done!' I give you full marks."

"I rehearsed a lot, you know," Kim confided.

Angier nodded. "I could tell you had. A smooth production takes lots of practice, and this was smooth as double Devon cream!"

"But who suggested the epilogue?" Malcolm queried. "Quite a shock to see fair Margaret shoving a bird in a bikini!"

"I thought it went well with the song," Kim said reflectively.

"Every playwright must settle with his own conscience how far to borrow from life." Angier rose, disappeared for a moment, and returned with a silver urn of long-stemmed crimson roses. He presented them to Kim with a courtly obeisance. "Congratulations, Kim! May all your first nights be as successful as this one!"

Dazed, Kim took the roses, stared up at her father and burst into tears.

"Here, here!" he said in dismay.

Kim put the extravagant flowers aside and gave him

166

a wild embrace. "I—I'm so happy I could die!" she laughed, tears like diamonds on her dark lashes.

"You're so happy you'll live a hundred years!" said Angier.

The evening finished with cakes and tea. Kim, though it was past her bedtime, was too joyously excited to get to sleep easily. She had her roses on a night stand pushed near the chaise, and she kept stroking the leaves.

"He gave them to me," she kept saying. "Angier gave them to me because my play was good. Supposing it had been bad, Eric? What would he have done with the flowers?"

"I'm sure I don't know," Erica smiled. "Maybe he'd have given them to Mrs. Shell."

"Not likely. I think he'd have given them to you. But this way we both have them, don't we, Eric? Oh, aren't they simply absolutely the most gorgeous things?"

"I never saw prettier," Erica said, with truth. "Now get to sleep or I'll have to go in some other room so you can drift off."

Kim sighed, cuddling the doll Lady Margaret as she nestled into her pillow. "This is the happiest day of my whole, whole life! There are these,"—she touched the roses a last blissful time—"and the play. And Angier kissed me! Twice!"

"That's lots to have sweet dreams on," Erica laughed. "Good night."

As was her usual custom after Kim was tucked in, Erica worked for a while on her thesis, showered, put on her gown and robe, and took one of the books she had to study and lay down with it across the bed. When she couldn't hold her eyes open, it would be time to sleep.

But her mind kept wandering from comparison of the elaborate court masques prepared by Ben Jonson and Inigo Jones for the court of James I, and folk plays like the ones centering around St. George which were rooted in ancient fertility rites.

Erica was, at the moment, more interested in the effects of the play Kim had put on that evening. She had obviously worked hard on it, which gave some grounds to think Angier had been right in mercilessly nipping off her earlier attempt to perform extemporaneously. And yet wasn't it a bit much for a nine-year-old to be held to professional effort and preparation before she could hope for a family audience?

Erica grimaced. Not many families contained a playwright of Angier's eminence! And Kim was probably the only child in the world who got long-stemmed roses in a silver urn for putting on a play with her dolls. It was all expressive of the wild extremes at Lady Gift; the outward quiet and natural beauty so different from the tormented web of relationships in the house that had one way or another led to Caitlyn's death.

Was it only a child's fascination with horror that had prompted Kim to show Caitlyn's death as murder? But ghosts didn't murder, even their staunchest believers stopped at that.

There was a rap at Erica's door, followed by a turning of the knob. Erica jumped up, slightly alarmed, and opened the door a crack.

"Kim's not in her bed," Peg gasped, wide brown eyes almost circular with fright. "The sheets are tossed about, but she's gone!"

What a nuisance! No way to calm Peg's fears except

the truth, which was bound to make her jealous. Erica widened the door enough for Peg to look through to the chaise where Kim slept beside her roses.

"Cor!" Peg breathed. She was plainly going to speak at length, with emphasis. Erica stepped into the gallery, shutting her door, and beckoned Peg what she hoped was a safe distance away.

"When Kim can't settle down, I let her sleep in my room," Erica explained. It wasn't necessary to say that this was every night. "I'd have told you, only it never occurred to me that you'd be upstairs this late."

"Are you forgetting I used to sleep outside her door every night?" demanded Peg. "Guarded her life like she was my very own, I did, but then you came along!" Peg leaned forward, color high, her placid bovine prettiness spoiled by outrage. "Now I'm just Peg from below stairs who'll serve to natter with when she's not busy with your ladyship!"

"Peg—"

"Don't Peg me!" the big girl almost wept. "Kimmie was my lamb! I had a care for her when no one else did, listened to her tales and kept her jolly! But now even that flint-hard daddy of hers pays her some attention, and I'm Peg Old-Clout!"

"Peg! Get hold of yourself! You are Kim's best, oldest friend. Nothing's going to change that."

"It is changed!"

"But you can't have wanted her to go on being ignored by her father!"

"Fine lot of good his notice is! Pushing her into trying like a slave to satisfy him, breaking her heart when she doesn't measure up! That's how Mrs. Shell says he did his wife. In a way he did the same to Miss St. Clair. And," warned Peg malevolently, lips peeling back from her teeth; "he'll do the same to you! You'll wind up dead like the others and—"

"Then Kim will have only you again, is that it?" Erica hardened her tone, sorry for the girl but repelled by her possessiveness. "Peg, I know—and appreciate—how you've looked after Kim. It is probably why she's stayed gay and high-spirited in spite of this house. But I have been employed to see to her, and that is primarily my responsibility. It will be much better and happier for all of us if you and I can get along."

"You mean it suits you to shift Kim off on me afternoons!"

"Peg, I will not put up with these tantrums."

"Oh, won't you now?" Peg's eyes gleamed and she set her hefty arms akimbo. "I'm to take your orders, am I?"

"Yes, if you want to put it that way!"

"And if I don't, you'll tattle to his High Mightiness!"

"Sleep on it, Peg. This isn't getting us anywhere."

"I think it is," said a deep voice from across the gallery. Both women whirled to see Angier coming toward them, massive in pajamas and robe.

XIV

Peg gave an impression of collapse, though she faced her master sturdily. "Peg," he said without heat, "I heard enough to conclude that we will have to do without your services. You may retain your flat till you find another position and you shall have two months' pay since I must give you such short notice."

"Sir—" faltered Peg, looking about like a large trapped hare. "Please, can't I—"

"I'm sorry."

Her eyes filled with tears. She turned blindly, groping for the rail.

Erica touched Angier's sleeve. He looked slowly down at her.

"Oh, please!" she murmured. "Please don't!"

"You want her to stay?"

"Yes."

He hesitated, shrugged, and called, "Peg!"

She turned, face touchingly hopeful. "Miss Hastings seems inclined to excuse you," he said. "We shall discuss it, and perhaps—mind you only perhaps—I will let you stay on if you think you can curb your tongue and remember that Miss Hastings is in absolute charge of everything to do with Kim. And that includes your duties."

"Yes, sir." Peg gave Erica a glance of mingled resentment and entreaty, bobbed her head, and escaped.

"Bit hard to have to hope someone you've attacked can save your job," Angier observed. "Now, Miss Hastings, where shall we contemplate this tempering of justice with mercy? Would you feel safer in your room than mine?"

"I feel perfectly safe anywhere," Erica said, stung to being less than honest. "But—Kim's sleeping in my room."

"Oh. So that was the cause of Peg's outrage! I will confess that I've found it a blessing not to find her crouched in front of Kim's room mornings like a human St. Bernard!" He motioned down the gallery. "Then, Miss Hastings, will you come into my quarters?"

She remembered her pajamas and robe. "Never mind," he counseled. "You're covered from chin to ankle, aren't you? I suppose," he continued conversationally, "that we both can't help being aware that those are the things you'll sleep in, and when one thinks of a lovely young woman sleeping—" He laughed, shut the door behind them and stood looking down at her. "Such dreams may come!"

He could no more keep from adding tension and fillip to a situation than a bird could keep from flying, Erica warned herself, retreating to a chair. She noticed that the beautiful mask had been removed from in front of his desk.

"I hope you'll give Peg another chance. There's no doubt that she loves Kim and has done all she could for her when—"

"When the father was scarcely doing his part?" finished Angier.

Erica flushed. "Peg is devoted."

"And very jealous."

"I think she'll get over that."

Angier moved his broad shoulders. "It's for you to decide. She can stay but on one condition."

"What?"

"You must not allow yourself to be subjected to any more such outbursts. Will you promise?"

"I don't intend to let Peg revile me! But tonight she was excited and forgot herself."

"Teach her to remember," Angier said.

Taking this as dismissal, Erica rose.

"Would you like a sherry?" he asked, moving toward the wall cupboard.

"No, thank you."

"Then sit with me while I have my nightcap," he coaxed. "It is not good for man to drink alone." He put down the bottle of Scotch and was beside her, taking her hands, before she could move. "That quote doesn't sound quite right, Miss Hastings. Where did I go wrong?"

Why did he play these games? Erica felt suddenly overwhelmingly tired, wanted only to go to her room and bed. But he was blocking her path, head tilted in that alert mocking way.

"It is not good for man to live alone," she corrected.

"Indeed? Who says so?"

"God!" she flashed. "In the book of Genesis!"

"I thought it had the ring of age and authority."

Out of patience, she started past him. His hands came down on her shoulders. "Erica! Don't mind my clowning, I always do it when I'm nervous!"

She stared at him incredulously. He, nervous with her? "You should see me opening nights!" he insisted, manner grave but eyes merry. "Erica, will you marry me?"

"What?"

"I hadn't expected quite so much shock! Dismay, perhaps, but—is it really such a surprise?"

"But—but—" She searched for something to convey her amazement. "You haven't even kissed me!"

"Not for lack of wishing!" He did, then, swiftly, so that to her increased confusion she was left longing for more. "Think!" he adjured her. "If I had wooed and blandished you without mention of marriage, wouldn't you have thought I was taking advantage of our positions and proximity?"

"Yes, but—"

"We haven't seen much of each other?"

"That's part of it," she said doggedly, shaken by that sweet, stirring, too brief kiss, still sure he was teasing, or in some way testing her.

"Erica—or must I go back to Miss Hastings? I'd call that hard to do with the woman I want so much to marry! Erica, you must take it from me that I have been in and out of love often enough in my forty years to judge my state. We are left with yours." He seated her in his big leather chair, lowered himself to the ottoman and set his chin in his hands. "Well, describe it."

"Describe what?"

"Your state, Erica! The state of your affections!"

"You can't be serious!"

"I am!"

"Then you might go about it differently!" Tears threatened and she fought them. "You—you seem to be playing a big joke!"

He dropped his pose and caught her hands. "Shall we be absolutely straightforward then? I love you. I love seeing you mother my child. I would be very proud if you would marry me." He laughed softly, his fingers on the pulse of her wrist so that she knew he could feel the racing of her blood. "How do you feel about me, Erica?"

"I—don't really know." His gaze compelled her to be truthful. "I find you tremendously exciting. I would like to know you were happy, but—"

"I'm moody, you don't like a lot of my attitudes, you wonder how any woman could possibly live with me! In short, you're afraid of what might happen if we married?"

Erica nodded. "And I don't know how Kim would take it."

He frowned, absently flexing her hands as if they were the most wonderful of intricate creations. "These are all valid points. But, Erica—tell me true! Are you troubled about what was between Caitlyn and me?"

"How can I help wondering? You must have loved her once, but I saw how you felt toward the end! Angier, I would rather die than have a man feel that way about me—guilty, angry, bound in spite of himself!"

His hands tightened on hers. He gave her a little shake. "Don't talk nonsense! You couldn't be like Caitlyn!" He sighed, lowered his voice. "Let me try to tell you how it was. I didn't love Caitlyn. After Kim's mother, I never expected to love again. You were a surprise, Erica, a not entirely welcome one till I began to enjoy the idea!" He flashed her a smile, then went on gravely, heavily, as if trying to be sure each word was true and fair.

"I didn't love Caitlyn, but I was infatuated by her, burned to possess her, and admired her great acting gifts. I made it clear from the start that there would be

175

no marriage. When I saw that she hoped for it anyway, I encouraged her to find other men. Two very wealthy ones did propose, but she turned them down. And then her career started downhill. I kept her solvent though we had long ceased to be lovers. I would always have done that gladly enough, but what I couldn't stand was her clinging! And she kept getting more and more strange. First she stopped eating meat, then she took up astrology, and she simply would not leave me in peace to do my work, on which, after all, both she and I depended!"

"It—it was terrible for you! And for her! And so sad." A bittersweet thought of Martin went through Erica's mind. If they had been lovers, would it have gone sour for them? Tears stung her eyes.

"What's the matter?" Angier's urgent touch brought her back to the present. He held her eyes searchingly. "Erica, do you have the faintest suspicion that I pushed Caitlyn?"

"I can't pretend that I haven't wondered. I've wondered about everyone in the house, including Kim, so you shouldn't be offended."

"I'm not, my darling. But will you wait for a certainty that may never come?"

"If you tell me you didn't kill her, I will believe you, Angier."

"Easily done. I didn't kill her."

"How can you be sure I didn't?"

His mouth quirked. "Love, aren't you forgetting? I've insisted from the start that it was suicide. Nothing has changed my mind. Now let's try for a summing up: it's only doubts of how we would get on together that keeps you from saying yes?"

Startled into laughter, she protested, "You make me sound so timorous!"

"You do have reasons! But don't forget," he charged solemnly, "that I, too, have occasion for caution!"

"Really?"

"Yes, indeed! Haven't you just coaxed me into retaining an impudent servant? Haven't you coerced me into spending a fortune on pruning old unthrifty trees? Haven't I been warned that if I want a family, I must put up with ice-lollies in my library and a general lot of racket? Are you not likely to want me to write masques instead of successful theater, while you behave like that truly fearsome thing, a literarily educated woman?"

Erica had to laugh. "But you proposed! I didn't!"

"True enough. But you must admit I've been handicapped in my wooing by fears of what you might think. Now that you are dismayed at how honorable and domestic my intentions are, I feel completely justified in storming you, courting you, blandishing you—doing anything I can to make you as ready as I am to enter into that perilous married condition."

"I can't believe you're serious—"

"Name a day."

"Oh, but—"

He laughed, rising, and lifting her to her feet with him. "You seem the one who's not serious—yet!"

This time his kiss was long; slow and sweet at first, then increasing to an urgency that shook her as she had never been shaken.

"Now," he said huskily, putting her at arm's length, "I shall walk you to your door like a proper suitor, and hope you will not sleep tonight for thinking of me!"

She raised a protesting hand, still feeling dazed. "Angier, I need time!"

"And you shall have it," he said, with a return to the courtliness she found irresistible. "But there's been too long without you! Don't make me wait any longer than you must."

"Angier—there's one thing more. How did Kim's mother die?"

"She crashed into the gate. A dog ran in front of her car. To avoid it, she hit the pillar." His face twisted. "She was impaled on the steering wheel."

"Then—she didn't die in the Old Orchard?"

"What makes you think that?" He frowned, then nodded. "Oh, because it was nettle-grown and you've seen me there a few times—Well, Erica, we walked there the night before she died; had a bloody quarrel. She had been an actress and felt as if she were stagnating in marriage. Next day she drove off for London. The orchard was the last place I saw her alive. Though I went there, I hated the place, too. But you've changed that."

So that was the secret of the orchard and the death of Kim's mother.

He walked Erica to her door, brushed a kiss on her cheek, and left her so abruptly that she looked after him with a pang of disappointment, almost called him back.

What nonsense! She couldn't hold him off with one hand and beckon with the other! They needed to know each other, spend time talking and seeing how they would match in other ways besides the rapturous intoxication he had revealed to her tonight.

Could he mean it? He must! Yet she could not really believe it, and deep in her heart she knew that it was this incredulity rather than any sane reasonable reservation that kept her from agreeing to marry him at once.

She woke to hear the rooks screeching on the lawn beneath the cedar of Lebanon. Early sun spilled through the window where Kim stood looking out.

"Cor! Cor!" went the crows. Kim turned, laughing.

"Now if they'd just say, 'Blimey!' wouldn't it be perfect?"

"They do strut about as if they owned the place," said Erica, going to stand by the child.

Had last night really happened? Erica wondered, gazing out past the sundial to the giant trees and the dainty little wych elm. She closed her eyes as her mouth remembered Angier's, as she felt his arms gathering her to him.

It had happened. Life had opened to her in that hour, dazzling, frightening, challenging, imperative. She loved him. If he loved her, there was no real choice to be made. But they did need time, and even more, Kim would. There could be no wedding till she welcomed the thought.

They did their yoga, beginning with the "Salutation to the Sun," which brought into play every muscle in slow pliant motions, ending with five minutes of deep breathing. They were still lying on the floor when Angier tapped and came in.

"How are my ladies this morning?" he asked, as they hastily scrambled up. "What is this, modern dancing?"

"It's yoga, Angier, to help my breathing!" Kim plopped down and reared her torso up without using her hands. "This is the Cobra! And I can do the Plough and Swan and Frog, too! Want to see me?"

179

"If there's such a menagerie housed in my daughter, I should know about it," Angier grinned. He watched, refraining from laughter when the Plough leaned very much to one side.

They went companionably along to breakfast. Angier's unwonted morning appearance caused a kitchen tizzy. He declined offers of deviled kidney and kippers, but tucked away two soft-boiled eggs, toast, and an orange, while Sybil studied him and Erica with a half-frown knitting her creamy brow.

"What brings the master forth betimes?" asked Malcolm, pouring a second cup of coffee. "You know, Angier, I can't remember ever seeing you this early in the morning?"

"Well, you do recognize me, don't you?" asked Angier, with slight pique.

"I'm not sure." Malcolm glanced from Angier to Erica, raised his eyebrows at her. "And you, Erica, you look unusually charming today! If one takes all these coincidences—"

"I'll save you making wrong deductions!" cut in Angier. "I have asked Erica to be my wife."

Kim gave a small startled cry, stared at Erica. Erica shot Angier a reproachful look, took Kim's hand and hurried out with her.

"Don't be upset, darling," Erica said reassuringly, the instant they were in her room. "Nothing is settled."

Kim caught her hands, blue eyes intent. "You will marry him, won't you?"

"Not unless and until you're happy about it." Erica's heart sank as she promised, making her realize how much she was already dreaming of a life with Angier. Yet she knew absolutely that Kim must welcome her into the marriage or it could not be.

Surely, with time and patience—

But would Angier have patience? Resentment at him for his precipitate exposure of their private affairs went hotly through Erica in the moment before Kim launched upward in a joyous hug.

"I am happy about it! Oh, Eric, please, please, do marry him! Then you'll never go away, will you?"

"Not unless you go, too," Erica managed, thrown off balance by this rapid acceptance. Was she the only one who needed time to get used to the idea?

Kim paced up and down, hugging herself in excitement. "Will you be my mother?" she asked abruptly.

"No. Kim. But I will act as if I were your mother, and love you as if I were. And I shall be your friend."

Kim reflected, dark brows mimicking Angier's scowl, and nodded. "That's good. I don't want a 'mother' mother—they're more for babies—but a friend will be super!"

"I'm glad to hear that," Angier said from the door. "Otherwise I'm afraid I would have started my courtship in stormy weather! So you approve of my taste, Kim?"

"Yes."

"And I suppose you want to be a bridesmaid and help pick the dresses and all that?"

"Oh, yes, please!" The glow in Kim's eyes grew even brighter. Angier gave Erica a wicked smile before blandly turning back to his daughter.

"And I suppose you think the sooner we entrap yon fair damsel the better? You don't think long engagements are a good idea?"

"They're horrid!" said Kim with vehemence.

"A proper engagement is just long enough to collect

a trousseau and get the rings. Right, Kim?"

She nodded, then looked at Erica, ran to her and said, "You must ask Eric, Angier! What she says is right!"

He groaned. "Betrayed! How can a poor man win when his women gang up?"

"You don't try to get around them," Kim advised, squeezing Erica's hand.

"Very well." Angier came forward, exaggerated repentance in his voice. "You have my daughter's consent, Erica. Now can't we have yours?"

"I'm sure no one was ever proposed to in such a way!" Erica protested in vexation and laughter.

"Still it's an earnest, serious proposal. You have to give an earnest, serious answer."

Erica looked from him to his daughter, who watched with her heart in her eyes, then said, smiling reluctantly. "Yes. I will marry you, Angier."

Kim clapped with excitement. "I—I'm going to tell Peg!" She rushed off. Angier closed the door and turned back to Erica in a way that showed he was no longer joking.

"Now I can kiss you!" he said.

And did.

XV

The wedding would be in three weeks. Angier had heavy business in London and was going up by himself for a few days to get through the urgent things. Then he would take Kim and Erica up to pick their dresses for the wedding. They would all attend the opening night of his new play before coming back to Lady Gift.

Erica had only two people who needed to know about her marriage. She telephoned the private hospital. Her mother's doctor said the older woman was much better, and that if Erica could take her home, and provide facilities for her to create her fantasy creatures, she might return to complete sanity. At any rate, she was not dangerous and longed to see Erica. Angier agreed that after the wedding, they would all fly to America and bring her mother back to live at Lady Gift. Kim was pleased at the thought of having a grandmother, and Erica hoped that her mother's life could be happier now than it had ever been.

Martin replied to her brief letter with a graceful, wry note of good wishes and a quote from Donne:

> *So if I dream I have you, I have you,*
> *For all our joys are but fantastical. . . .*

Sybil was courteous but seemed under strain. Mrs. Shell and the dailies fluttered and cooed. Peg gave Erica many rebellious glances, though she was verbally dutiful. Malcolm watched them all with his oblique, hooded gaze.

"I wish you connubial bliss," he told her, after Angier announced their engagement at dinner the same day he had told of his proposal. "If you have it with Angier, you'll earn it!"

"I think one earns any happiness," said Erica, and knew how prim she sounded even before Malcolm chortled, pulled his bronze forelock, and kissed her hand.

"Don't mind me, Erica! I'm just a little sorry to give up all hopes of you myself. You sympathize with that, don't you, Sybil?"

"I hope everyone will be happy," Sybil said, without expression. Rising quickly, she muttered an excuse, and left the table.

Angier looked stormy.

"There's some sorting out to do," Malcolm remarked. "I never have really thought having one's ex-wife as a secretary was a good idea, old chap."

"If we start having moods, there will be some sorting out," Angier promised.

But there were no direct clashes or scenes, though Angier and Malcolm carried most conversation at meals, interspersed with Kim's chatter.

Erica felt as if she were floating in a dream. To be loved by Angier Matthews, to be mistress of Lady Gift and make it come alive and joyful with family and friends! She and Angier would have children, of course, but she could not love them more than Kim, who had for so long been the only light in this great house.

Even Erica's mother would have a place here, with a nurse if necessary. The closed end of the summer pavilion was being converted to a studio with a kiln. Working there, being able to look out across the Old Orchard, would surely bring much peace to the older woman.

Erica had one self-appointed task to finish before the wedding. She wanted to complete the outline of her thesis. It might be several months before she settled down to it again, and the outline would serve to hold facts that were presently fresh in her mind.

The day Angier started up to London, Erica and Kim waved him off. After finishing their lessons and having lunch, Peg took Kim to the pool while Erica settled with her books. She became absorbed in the quarrel between Jones and Jonson over which had made the greatest contribution to the masques, and lost track of time till Malcolm's voice made her whirl toward the open door.

"Erica, have you seen Kim?"

"Isn't she with Peg?"

"Peg can't find her. Obviously Peg was dandling with our young blond gardener in one of the sheds, and when she came out, Kim was gone."

A constricting band of fear closed around Erica's heart. Why hadn't she paid more attention to the time? Or been emphatic with Peg about concentrating on Kim when they were together?

"How long has Kim been missing?"

"Not long. She probably got bored with waiting on Peg and went off on her own. I thought for sure she'd be with you."

"Where have you looked?" demanded Erica, remembering that other time Kim had vanished and the wearing fruitless search for her.

"Peg's hunting around the grounds and Clock House. I came through the butler's pantry and ducked through the library and sun room."

"She might have gone to the roof. Of course, she was warned not to go by herself."

"That wouldn't stop our Kimberley if she set her head to go," Malcolm laughed. "I'll have a peek, shall I, and let you know?"

"I'll come!" Erica hurried down the gallery ahead of Malcolm. "I'm sure she's perfectly all right, but I'm nervous!"

They went up the ladder and along the catwalk to the window, which hung partly open. Malcolm gave Erica's hand a squeeze. "Looks as if we're in luck," he said, letting her precede him.

As she stepped out on the roof and sighted Peg and Kim lazing in the sun, Erica smiled in relief. "Peg's found her!" she called, turning to Malcolm.

What she saw almost made her lose her balance. Malcolm held a gun. "Don't be afraid of slipping, my dear." His small, even teeth had never looked so white. "It's only a matter of minutes." He raised his voice imperatively. "Just stay quiet, Peg!"

He went on conversationally, in a tone of gentle regret. "For both our sakes, Erica, I wish you had been inclined to my wooing. But Sybil and I have invested too much—our lives, in fact, in Angier. We can't let our shares go to a wife, however charming."

Erica moved her head in dazed bewilderment.

"You pushed Caitlyn," she faltered. But the words didn't sound true. This couldn't be happening!

Malcolm nodded. "She had a share of Angier, too, and since the poor girl was suicidal, it seemed permissible to help her along." His gaze followed Erica's to Peg and Kim. Peg's eyes bulged with fear. Her large bosom rose and fell heavily but she kept an arm tightly around Kim, who didn't seem to understand what was happening.

"I'd like to leave Kimberley out of this," said Malcolm, "but Sybil points out that so long as the child is around, Angier will always have thoughts of giving her a mother. A tragedy like this should blight him forever, don't you think? He'll cleave to his faithful secretary and accountant. As long as he produces, he can live. But when he starts living on his savings, a suicide should be simple to arrange for a man who has endured so many griefs."

"It—it can't be!" Erica whispered. It seemed that the still golden air must move and shatter this nightmare.

Malcolm flashed a smile. He looked handsome and burnished in the sun, almost young. "When the cat's away, the mice will play. Ever since Angier left, we've been watching for a chance to get the three of you on the roof at the same time. Sybil's downstairs to intercept Angier if he should happen home before the tragedy. But I don't suppose he will. And if he did come now and force us to kill him, we could make it look like suicide over your tragic death."

Kim observed Malcolm with what seemed more interest than fright. She probably couldn't really believe him. "You are a hypercrite," she decided.

"Hypocrite, dear," Malcolm corrected.

Peg, ungainly in her bikini, scrambled toward the man. Tears poured down her cheeks as she fell on her knees. "Kill me, but let Kimmie go!"

Malcolm shoved her back with his foot. "You poor cow," he said pityingly. "You've given us the way to make this wholesale tragedy plausible! Mrs. Shell and the gardeners have heard you say you wished Erica would take the same tumble Caitlyn did. Everyone knows how wild you are about Kim. What could be more natural, after two witnesses, Sybil and I, heard Erica discharge you, than your luring Erica on the roof and pushing her off?"

"But Kim—" protested Erica.

"She was either a jealous little girl who helped do you in, or she struggled to protect you so that when you and Peg fell struggling to your deaths, you swept her with you." He actually smiled at Kim, who was beginning to look frightened and moved closer to Erica. "At least, old girl, you'll have a fitting hecatomb of two young women!"

Erica's mind had been flashing in search of some hope, blanking out when each glimmering idea had to be discarded. But one fact suddenly shone clear.

Their deaths had to look like falling. A bullet in any of them would call for explanations. Malcolm didn't want to shoot.

Besides, what was there to lose?

Apparently, deep in her country brain, Peg came to the same conclusion. She hurled herself forward, striking Malcolm heavily in the legs. He staggered wildly, aimed. Erica knocked up his arm. He went all the way off balance, fired wildly, and fell.

There was one cry, then a sound of soft weight striking with great force. Erica's legs gave way. She sank down by the gasping Peg, shaking uncontrollably. Kim crept over to them and huddled in between.

No sound came from below. After a moment, Peg eased over, looked, and nodded. "He's done."

"But Sybil's still downstairs," Erica said. "And she probably has a gun. I wonder if she heard that shot."

"Everyone must have, but they might think it was one of the gardeners picking off a few pigeons."

"Sybil will know better! We've got to be fast. Peg, you take Kim over behind the chimney. Stay there till I come back or send you word it's all right."

"Oh!" wailed Kim, clinging to her. "She may kill you!"

"She may kill all of us if we don't move! Go with Peg, and keep quiet!"

Even if Sybil did get up on the roof, she would have to walk out some distance in order to see the pair. That would give Peg a chance to take her by surprise. *But I'll stop her!* Erica thought grimly, climbing down to the catwalk. In the dim light, she looked around for a weapon.

There was none. She would just have to hurry down and try to get help or ambush Sybil with some kind of clubbed object. . . . Erica's foot was on the second rung of the ladder when someone below gripped it.

She froze. Dizzy with terror, she gazed down, choked in relief and almost tumbled into Angier's arms.

He held her close but forced up her chin as if to snap her into consciousness. "Erica! That shot—"

"Sybil! She—she may have a gun!"

"She did. And she's dead! I came back early to surprise you. She was in the library with a lot of questions. We heard a shot. When I started to look, she pulled the gun. We wrestled for it and she took the bullet. Now what went on up there?"

"Let's go tell Kim and Peg it's safe," Erica urged. But she melted in his arms, so relieved and weak that he had to help her start moving again.

At first Angier could scarcely believe that his associates of years had so cold-bloodedly set out to protect their profits from him.

"I suppose when Helen died, they thought they would be my main heirs provided I didn't marry again," he mused. "Sybil must have felt that as first wife and secretary she was entitled to a large share of my estate." His eyes burned. "What I can't get over is how they could kill Kim. They've known her since she was born! I was certainly their goose laying golden eggs! And I was convinced that poor Caitlyn had killed herself—"

"It's all over," Erica reminded. "We'll make Lady Gift such a happy place that all the ghosts will leave!"

Those moments of shared danger on the roof, and their joint success in overcoming Malcolm and saving Kim and themselves, had taken much of the rub out of Erica's and Peg's relationship. The night of their terror on the roof, Peg had come to Erica and sheepishly confessed that she had been the "ghost" who had frightened previous nannies and companions.

"They were no good for Kimmie," the big girl finished defiantly. "I thought the sooner they were on their way, the better! And it didn't take much to send 'em—a few silly noises and tweaks! But Miss, I'm truly glad you'll be Kimmie's mum! And you may rely on me to always back you up, just like I did on the roof!" And she scuffed away with a self-righteous tilt to her head.

Peg made the most of her glory. A few days later, Erica heard Kim praising her. "You're a real heroine, Peg! If you hadn't lunged for Malcolm the way you did, he'd have shoved us all off. Erica says she couldn't have stopped him by herself."

"It took both of us, poppet," Peg said, hugging the child tight. "And you remember, if your mum and I could handle a killer, we can manage a saucy puss like you!"

Erica smiled to herself. It was going to be a new, bright life for them all. She knocked on Angier's door. It seemed a lifetime ago that she had first walked through it.

Angier opened. His dark brows rushed together in a scowl that reminded her laughably of the first time they met.

"Of all the cheek!" he scolded, holding her at arm's length. "Don't you dare knock on my door again! Soon, you know, it's going to be yours, too!"

"I'll try to remember," Erica said. Then she met his kiss and they both forgot everything but each other.

PRINTING AFTER PRINTING IN HARDCOVERS

NOW A BERKLEY PAPERBACK—

THE VITAL AND DRAMATIC STORY OF

ROSE FITZGERALD KENNEDY

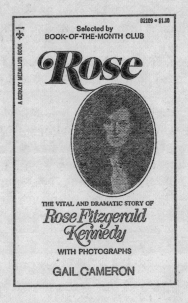

ROSE, by Gail Cameron   (D2109—$1.50)

"The best portrait of Rose we are likely to get."—*Life*

Send for a *free* list of all our books in print